AT THE
CORNER OF
6TH AND NORTH

Joshua J McNeal

WESTBOW
PRESS
A DIVISION OF THOMAS NELSON

Scripture quotations taken from the New American Standard Bible®, Copyright © 1960, 1962, 1963, 1968, 1971, 1972, 1973, 1975, 1977, 1995 by The Lockman Foundation. Used by permission." (www.Lockman.org)

WestBow Press books may be ordered through booksellers or by contacting:

WestBow Press
A Division of Thomas Nelson
1663 Liberty Drive
Bloomington, IN 47403
www.westbowpress.com
1-(866) 928-1240

ISBN: 978-1-4497-1697-4 (sc)
ISBN: 978-1-4497-1698-1 (dj)
ISBN: 978-1-4497-1696-7 (e)

Library of Congress Control Number: 2011928145

Printed in the United States of America

WestBow Press rev. date: 6/6/2011

Chapter 1

"My love for you overwhelms me! And I can keep quiet..."
Wham!

"That shut ya up!" shouted Diana as she shut off her radio rather forcefully. Embarrassment suddenly swept over her as she realized how immature she had just acted. She took a quick glimpse into the rearview mirror to see if her kids had noticed. John, the oldest, just stared out the side window with his earphones in, as he always did. Her daughter, Kara, met her eyes and looked very confused.

Diana quickly asked, "Kara, what are you going to do at your dad's this weekend?"

"I don't know. Most of the time we just watch TV. I really hope he will take us to the zoo. I've been begging him for so long. I really want to see the white tiger."

"You love tigers, don't you, hon?" Diana winked.

Kara just looked at her and smiled.

—

She cried most of the way home, as she did every time she dropped off her children. Thunder rumbled in the distance as a storm approached. She glared at the quickly darkening sky and released a sigh.

"You would rain on me now."

She pulled into her driveway and turned off the engine. The tapping of rain on the roof of her Sedan drowned out her sobs. Diana sat there, not wanting to move. A close flash of lightning lit up her car and made her jump. The vibration of her phone caused a slight scream to escape from her lips.

"How ya doing, darling?" Her best friend, Lisa, always knew when to call.

"How do you think I'm doing?" Diana responded through her sniffles. "I had to leave my two babies with a man I'm married to and not living with, all that's on the radio are love songs, it's pouring, and I'm going to be alone all night."

"You should try the country station. I hear there aren't as many love songs there," Lisa said, chuckling. "And I think Duke is great company."

Diana couldn't help but laugh. She could see her beagle peeking between the curtains already waiting for her to come and give him food and a good belly rub.

"I just don't know what to do. Everything is slowly collapsing around me. I feel claustrophobic everywhere I go. My life is slowly sucking the life out of me."

Lisa calmed her down as only she could do. "I've been praying for you, love. Please come to church with me this weekend. It's at least something to do to keep your mind occupied as you wait for your kids to come back."

"I don't know," she said and sighed. "I appreciate the offer, like always. It's just not for me. But if there is a chance that it will help, you have my permission to keep praying."

Lisa laughed. "Oh, you can count on it. I love you. Stay strong, okay?"

"I love you, too. I will do my best."

—

Attacking her feet, Duke made her almost fall headlong into the house. His panting and bouncing were too overwhelming for her current mood.

"Duke! Down!" The surprised dog backed off, whimpering. He ran to his bed, slightly shaking, and plopped down.

"I'm sorry, boy," Diana apologized, bending down and scratching him behind his left ear. "Today is not a happy day. Here, let me get you a biscuit."

After making amends, which included a bowl of fresh water, a heaping pile of Kibbles, and a belly scratch that lasted longer than usual, she settled into her hot tub and stared at the storm just beyond the screen that protected her from the downpour.

She wished there was a screen that was between her and her circumstances. If only there were a barrier that could protect her from the pain that was continually beating her down. She felt like a defeated, bleeding boxer sitting in his corner unable to stand. Tears welled up again, but she was too tired to cry. She was too tired to do anything. Her head fell back against the edge of the sauna, and her eyes closed.

Memories suddenly invaded her mind. She pictured the red brick church where her mom had taken her every week. She could smell the dampness of the basement and hear the booming voice of Reverend Kennedy. Her mom would sit straight backed next to her, leaning on every word. She remembered drawing pictures of various exotic animals where sermon notes should have been. She loved them as much as Kara did now. But the drawing was always interrupted by the sharp elbow of her irritated mother.

She thought about her father. He had been a great provider, putting in fifty hours a week at the lumber mill. But as for being a dad, he hadn't done much. He never attended any of her ballet recitals or choir concerts and certainly never church. If he wasn't at work, he was either in his La-Z-Boy with a beer or in bed snoring. The memories of him caused tears once again to make trails down her cheeks.

Thoughts of her wedding created more tears. Jim had looked so handsome in his black tux with that glow in his eyes that she had grown to love. She remembered the feeling when he had kissed her at the altar. In his embrace, nothing could hurt her. She had felt protected from the world right there in his arms. His voice whispered in her ear, "You look gorgeous. I love you so much." Butterflies formed in her stomach once again, just as they had when he'd first said the words sixteen years before.

Jim towered over her at six foot five, causing her to look shorter than she really was. His hair was black, and hers was blond. His eyes were dark brown while hers were light blue. Jim had been born in Virginia while she was from Colorado. Nothing about their pasts, looks, or personalities were the same. They were the golden example of opposites attracting. Nobody would have guessed that they would have fallen in love, but from the moment they took their seats next to each other in Geology 102, they were inseparable. A flood of memories filled her mind. She recalled starlit walks beside the river hand in hand and long talks over coffee and cinnamon rolls. She remembered the ski resort where he placed that glimmering ring on her finger.

She shook out of her daydream and into the realization that the rain had stopped. The pleasant smell of the crisp air invaded her nostrils, and she carefully got out of the hot tub. She stood looking out past the screen as she dried herself. Darkness had taken over, and she couldn't see anything past the streaming rays of the porch light. She seemed to be standing in a very illustration of her own existence, except in her life, the light was much dimmer.

As she heated an instant bowl of oatmeal in the microwave, she wished tomorrow would stay far away. She hated her days off when her children were gone somewhere. She knew it would be like every other day that was similar. Ignoring the time and staying in bed until very late, she would shower longer than normal, maybe go for an afternoon jog, and then return home for the rest of the day, lying in wait for the return of her kids. It was a miserable time but one she had learned to live with. John had been a struggle ever since he hit puberty, always wanting to be with friends instead of with her and hibernating in his room when he was home. But she still loved him dearly and tried to treasure each moment she could with him. It was much easier to relax knowing he was upstairs than to think of him across town in another house. And there was dear, sweet Kara. She was a spitting image of her father, tall for her age and smart as well. She had just entered the fifth grade and was already excelling. Diana hoped it would be at least another couple of years before she started rebelling too.

Maybe she never will, Diana thought. *Wouldn't that be wonderful?*

The shrill ring of the telephone caused a short gasp to leave her throat. She stumbled over to the phone, quickly pulling it to her ear.

"Hello?"

"Hello, Mrs. Newman?"

"Um, yes. Who is this?" she questioned. Leaning against the counter, she furrowed her brow in confusion. Who could be calling at this hour?

"Yes, Mrs. Newman, this is a very good friend of Lisa's. She has been asking us to meet for some time now. I have helped her through a lot, and she thought our meeting would be a good idea."

"Lisa wants us to meet?" she asked.

"Yes. So tomorrow you are going to get an invitation in the mail. It will have a time and place where you will come to meet me. I will provide you with a place to stay where you will get the much-needed rest you have been longing for. I will also present you with a fantastic gift, if you will only come and receive it."

"How do I know that this is not a hoax or you aren't some kind of creep trying to abduct me?" Her guard was rising, and she found herself gnawing on her middle finger.

"I know that you have seen a change in Lisa over the past few years. Her anger and resentment have subsided, and she has become a much happier and more pleasant person to be around. All I will leave you with is this question: do you want a change in your life? The invite will be in your mailbox tomorrow. It's your choice. Have a nice night, Diana."

And with that, the phone line went dead. She stood in her kitchen with the phone still in her hand for many minutes reviewing the past conversation in her head. She quickly dialed Lisa's phone number, but her phone quickly went to voicemail.

Her mind was racing as she changed into her pajamas and brushed her teeth. She lay in bed lost in thought for a long time before drifting off to sleep.

—

Not long after sunrise, she awoke to Duke scratching at the door downstairs needing to go outside. She threw on her robe and ran down the steps. Grabbing the pink leash off the coat rack next to the door, she hooked it on Duke's collar and walked out into the sunshine and freshness of a new day. She smiled as she thought back to the day they'd bought Duke. The pet store owner, Ted, had assured them that the puppy was a girl so Kara, only seven at the time, picked the nice pink leash. Jim and Diana were both huge "Dukes of Hazard" fans, and hence, couldn't name the dog anything but Daisy. It wasn't until the dog's next appointment that the truth came out and Daisy became Duke.

Duke started on his normal routine, first sniffing the air and then circling the yard, looking for that perfect spot. The neighborhood glowed in the aftermath of the rain. Diana watched a couple trying to stuff three little kids into a minivan across the street. It was humorous to watch the two flustered parents and the three excited, uncooperative children. She could hear the father yelling that they wouldn't go at all if they didn't get in the car and the children saying that they couldn't wait until they got there. She didn't know where they were going, but she knew two things for sure: the kids were more excited than the parents, and mom and dad would sleep very well tonight.

The beagle yanked on his leash, signifying that he was finished and hungry. Stooping down to pick up the newspaper, Diana followed Duke back into the house for breakfast. Every morning without the kids consisted of the same pity breakfast: two over-easy eggs, three strips of bacon, two charred pieces of toast, and a tall glass of cold, refreshing orange juice. Duke also received an extra chicken-flavored biscuit on these mornings.

A jog seemed only appropriate as restlessness sunk in. She hated every day without her kids, and this day seemed to be dragging on slower than normal. She changed into her normal jogging outfit that consisted of yellow shorts rising above the knee and a yellow and blue–striped tank top.

She hooked up Duke once again, and he began to bounce around the room immediately. She could barely get her shoes tied as the beagle ran around her, continually trying to get right up in her face.

"Duke, we can't leave unless you settle down for a minute," she pleaded. "Just let me get my shoes on!"

Once out the door, the dog knew his routine; don't run too far ahead and to the side. He knew his place right beside her. She turned left at the end of her driveway and headed west down Sycamore Street. They had moved here nine years ago when Jim had received a great opportunity as a building contractor, the career of his dreams. For the most part, she liked the small neighborhood. She couldn't say that she knew too many people who lived around her, but they were quiet and courteous, and to Diana, that was the most important thing.

The sun beat down as she ran. She quickly remembered her water bottle still sitting on the ledge by her door.

Looking down at Duke, she uttered, "This will be a shorter jog than normal, buddy. We don't want to die of heat exhaustion."

Duke seemed to agree as he trudged on next to her and felt the intense heat of the sun. It was a beautiful day. Diana could only see one small cloud up through the trees that surrounded her. Squirrels were darting to and fro in front of her. She often wondered what they were truly up to. They always seemed so busy.

Diana suddenly stopped and could barely get the words out. "Oh why did I go this way …"

The brick house loomed behind the picket fence. It stared her down and taunted her. The sweat running down her face was soon mixed with tears as she stood lifeless before the estate. She hated this house. The only thing she disliked about this whole neighborhood was this place.

She glared at the front door. "I hate you. You ruined my life."

Turning around quickly, she raced back to her own home. Stopping at her mailbox, she grabbed the mail and headed back inside. Duke went straight for his water bowl and lapped loudly, desperately trying to hydrate.

She quickly took a shower and pulled herself back together. The last thing she needed today was haunting memories. Returning downstairs, she sifted through the mail. The many doubts in her head that she would find an invitation among the junk mail and bills suddenly vanished as she held in her hand a small envelope with only her name and address on the front.

Diana tore it open, and sure enough, a card with a time and place was inside.

She read aloud. "The corner of Sixth and North at 7:00 p.m. … today? This invite is for today! That's crazy! Talk about last minute."

She opened the cupboard door under the sink to throw it away when something else in the envelope caught her eye. She removed a photo and had to catch herself on the counter. Her eyes scanned a picture that she had never seen before, but the first glance at it almost made her faint.

She stared at a photo of her father holding a tiny baby wrapped in a yellow and white blanket. She knew immediately it was her. So many emotions filled her at once; she didn't know how to feel. He was much younger and very handsome, with his buzz cut and quirky smile. His face gleamed, as he seemed so proud in that moment.

No memories that she had with her father ever consisted of him holding her. But this photo showed him doing the exact thing she longed for her entire childhood.

She closed the cupboard door and set the photo and invitation back onto the counter. Her gaze hopped back and forth from the invite to the mysterious picture.

The grandfather clock in the living room chimed 10:00 a.m. Looking back at the contents on the counter, she sighed. She had to decide whether she was going to meet this mysterious stranger.

Rest would be nice, she thought.

Dialing Lisa's number, she again only got a voicemail. Running her hands through her hair, she took a deep breath. She had nine hours to figure out what she wanted to do.

Chapter 2

"I shouldn't be gone too long, baby. I'm just going away for a little while. I promise I'll be back in time to pick you up from your dad's."

She paused. "Oh, I'm so glad he's taking you to the zoo! That's wonderful! Have fun, Kara. I love you!"

Diana hung up and leaned against a light pole, closed her eyes, and took a deep breath. She opened her eyes and read her cell phone: 6:46. She was never known to be a risk taker. In fact, she'd avoided anything that she was unsure about. She had quit church as soon as she could make her own decisions. Believing in something she couldn't see seemed very foolish. She'd never bought lottery tickets, had never moved away, and had the same job as a bank teller for twenty-two years. In fact, the only risk she had ever taken was to get married.

What am I doing? she thought. *This is crazy!*

But something inside her wouldn't allow her to turn away. She could see the meeting place two blocks away from where she was standing. An old three-story building loomed above her corner destination. She could barely read the dimly lit sign next to it but made out the words: *The People's Pawn Shop.* A Starbucks stared at the old building from across the street, bragging about how good it looked.

Seated against a public trash bin was a bearded man. The only way she knew he was alive was by the movement of his head, which followed every vehicle that passed in front of him. Walking toward him on the crosswalk was a young lady, probably mid-twenties, pushing a yellow umbrella stroller. From behind the seated man approached another, but he was dressed very nicely in a red collared shirt and black slacks. He looked in every direction while peeking at a pocket watch he held in his left hand.

It was 6:49. Diana took one last deep breath and starting walking toward the corner. She kept an eye on the three strangers ahead of her, being very cautious. What she was getting herself into? From behind her, a white Jaguar roared up carelessly, pulling up to the curb and barely missing a parked black Sedan. The nicely groomed white-haired man who appeared out of the driver's side was sporting a bright Hawaiian-colored shirt and tan khaki shorts. His hand tightly gripped a briefcase. He took one look at the dirty, bearded man near the garbage can and stepped back a few steps and then calmly looked at his watch. It seemed that this was becoming a common trend among the group.

Diana offered all four a small smile as she too joined the group. There was a very awkward silence as each kept to themselves. She noticed the same invite sticking out of the back pocket of the nicely dressed man.

"Excuse me, sir. I don't want to sound nosy, but are you here because you received a phone call?"

"Well, ma'am," he sneered, "unfortunately, that did sound nosy."

She could feel her face get warmer and stumbled over what to say next.

"I'm sorry," she apologized, "but I have to wonder if that card is why you are standing here right now."

He turned and faced her and looked her up and down. A weird look appeared on his face as he reached back and grabbed the invitation out of his pants pocket. He eyed the rest of the crowd, who all seemed very attentive to the conversation.

"How do you know about the phone call?" he asked accusingly. "Did you send me this? Do you know who did?"

"Wait," she quickly backtracked. "The only reason I know about it is because I got one too!"

She pulled her card out of her coat pocket and held it up for him to see. He looked at hers intensely and quickly apologized.

"I'm sorry. I just want to know what this is all about. Somebody called me last night at exactly 10:00 saying they were a friend of a friend."

Diana's thoughts raced as she realized their phone calls happened at the exact same time. She looked at the young woman who met eyes with her.

"Did you receive one too?" Diana asked her.

The woman looked at her with scared eyes and nodded. The bearded man looked up from his curbside seat, nodding and waving an envelope. They all fell silent again. The only thing that they could hear was the traffic that continued around them and a few birds chirping in a tree nearby.

"It's 6:59," the rich white-haired man said in a low, barely audible voice.

They all waited silently the final minute. To Diana, that last minute felt like hours. Fear gripped her for the first time since she'd arrived at the corner. She felt a slight comfort in knowing that she wasn't alone, but the mystery grew even deeper because of the four other people waiting here beside her.

The beeping of the old man's watch made her jump, causing the other lady to jump as well.

"All right, where is—"

Before the red-shirted man could finish his question, the squealing of well-used brakes made them spin around. A school bus parked next to the curb, and its door immediately opened. The driver was an elderly black man with a full white beard. He wore a black suit, a tie, and a beret.

He turned to the confused crowd standing speechless on the sidewalk, gave them a big smile, and yelled, "Hop on! It's time to roll!"

—

Pulling the last bed sheet tight, the hotel owner finished making the final bed. He had spent the last three hours preparing rooms for the guests that he hoped would be arriving in a few minutes. Every room was impeccable. He was ready.

Checking dinner one more time and making sure each dish was perfectly set on the dining room table, the owner headed out the back door. Walking up the mountain, he sat down and buried his head in his hands. Before they arrived, he needed to spend time interceding.

—

"What do you mean hop on?" the lady with the baby questioned. "I came for a gift. Where's my gift?"

The red-shirted man piped in, "Yeah! I'm not getting on that bus. I don't have time for this. I told my wife I was just running to the store to pick up a gallon of milk and some stamps. I can't leave on some unmarked school bus to who knows where!"

The driver looked at them both. "If you don't come, you will not receive your gift. Please get on the bus. I promise you will not be missed."

The homeless man pushed through the crowd and climbed the steps onto the bus. He relied heavily on the driver's outstretched hand. Diana saw standing off to herself a very young girl observing the whole scene. She wore a low-cut white shirt and a very short black skirt with matching knee-high boots. In her hand, she held a guitar case, along with a notebook tucked underneath her arm. She seemed very leery of all that was going on.

The man in the red shirt continued to argue with the driver. "Listen, I didn't come here for some joyride. I just want you to give me the name of the punks who have been sending crank calls. If you won't, I ask that you at least tell them to stop or I will be forced to call the police."

The bus driver laughed. "Sir, the police have no authority where he is. If you would please hurry and get on, he is waiting."

Diana's heart was racing. Everything in her wanted to believe that this bus was going to take her to a place that could truly give her the rest that she desired. She could see the dirty bearded man looking out the front seat window at the rest of the group.

The rich Jaguar owner sighed loudly. "Aah, I have nothing to lose. Get out of the way."

And with that, he entered the bus and took his seat near the middle. Diana finally decided the risk was worth the offer despite her better judgment and climbed the steps. She expected something different when she boarded, but what she found was an ordinary old school bus. The green seats were torn in many places, and the floor had numerous stains on it. One of the windows was at a cockeyed angle and stuck halfway down. She found a seat on the other side of the aisle from the other two men, three seats from the back.

The driver looked at the three still standing outside. "Charles, Madison, and Courtney, we need to go now. Get on the bus."

The color drained from their faces. Diana watched intently as Charles pointed his finger nervously and glared at the man.

"How do you know my name?"

The bus driver smiled politely. "Come and find out, my friend. My name is Chester."

With that quick introduction, Chester reached out his hand to Madison. The woman with the baby walked up the steps, carefully eyed the driver as she walked by, and gently sat two seats in front of Diana.

"This is the last call," Chester continued. "All aboard!"

Charles took one last look around him at nothing in particular, ran his hand through his blond, curly hair, and walked toward the bus. He took one glance back at the girl who stood there frozen in fear and then entered the vehicle. The girl took one step backward from the curb.

"Now, Courtney, you know you need to get on, don't you? Don't be afraid. I promise nobody will hurt you."

Courtney listened as Chester pleaded with her. Her frightened face never changed, but she slowly started taking steps toward the bus. She stopped just before the door.

"I have to be back by tomorrow night," she finally spoke.

The driver nodded. "You will be."

—

Diana sat through the silent part of the trip slouching in her seat and staring out the window. Familiar businesses and landmarks passed her by as the bus took her away from life as she knew it. Second thoughts returned, and she peered up at the driver, who concentrated fully on the busy traffic that surrounded him. A little girl strapped into a car seat looked up at Diana from within the white minivan parked beside them at a stop light and pointed at her, smiling. Diana waved at her and thought about her own little girl.

What am I doing? she thought, shaking her head.

Her worries were quickly interrupted by Charles again prodding Chester for answers.

"Hey, Chester, where are we going? Do you know who sent the invitations? How did you know where I lived?"

Chester grinned into his rearview mirror and then returned his attention to the road.

The homeless man turned around and glared at Charles. "Quit asking questions. We'll find out soon enough."

"Hey, pal, I really don't think I was talking to you!" Charles shot back. "Turn around and shut up. If I want a remark from you, I'll precede my question with, 'Hey, bum!'"

The dirty bearded man immediately stood and looked Charles up and down. Diana could see his fists tightening and his knuckles turning white. The last thing she needed was a brawl only feet away from her on this bus. She was already regretting getting on.

Charles was now standing and continuing to yell like an elementary boy trying to act tough in front of his friends on the playground.

"What, you gonna punch me! I know this mystery bus trip is exciting for you since you have nothing, but I have a career and a family. I need to know if I'll be back soon."

The man's fists remained tight, and his eyes moved from anger to sadness. He stepped toward Charles, muttering words under his breath. Charles started walking toward the bearded man, whose right eye began to form a tear. The rich man stood up between them and extended his arms, stopping their progress.

"That's enough manliness from both of you," he commanded. "Sit down and be quiet. None of us know what is going on, and fighting amongst each other isn't going to help anything. I want to know just as much as you do, but we are going to have to wait."

The dirty bearded man returned to his seat, favoring his knee again as he sat. The wealthy Jaguar driver slowly lowered himself back to his seat between the two men but his eyes never left Charles. Charles's attention was darting from the rich man to the bearded man, up to Chester, and back to the rich man. His hands loosened, and he took a long, deep breath.

With a deep grunt, he returned to his seat. Diana's eyes met his, and she forced a smile. The baby started crying. Madison picked up her infant, leaned it against her shoulder, and starting bouncing it. The bearded man looked back.

"What's the baby's name?"

"Fern," she answered.

"Fern," the man repeated. "That's nice. How did you come up with that name?"

Madison's attention was on the bearded man seated across the vehicle from her. Fern had stopped fussing and was now looking back toward Diana. She had grabbed Madison's collar, placed it into her mouth, and proceeded to suck on it.

"Why do you ask?" Madison questioned.

The man looked surprised by the question. His eyes darted to the other passengers, as if he was looking for any kind of help in his predicament.

"I don't know," he mumbled. "Isn't that a common question that people ask about babies? My parents named me Louis after my grandfather. I wasn't trying to pry …"

"I made it up," Madison interrupted. "Okay? I made it up."

Louis nodded slightly, still looking shocked. He turned around and faced forward. The atmosphere in the vehicle was very tense. Diana realized that she had chewed her thumb nail down so much that it started to ache. Overwhelming temptations to stop the vehicle and get off hounded her. These people were crazy. There was the quiet young girl named Courtney who never looked up. And there was softhearted Louis who looked and smelled like he hadn't bathed in many weeks. Quick-tempered Charles sat leaning back staring at the ceiling. There was the rude mother, Madison, and her daughter, Fern. And last there was the rich old man eyeing each person as well. She again wished that she had never responded to the invitation.

She jumped as the rich man plopped down in the seat next to her, sporting an oversized grin. He offered his hand to her.

"My name is Harvey. What's yours?"

"Diana," she answered, shaking his hand.

He continued, "You have been pretty quiet this whole time. You seem really nervous or really shy."

She straightened up. "Well, there is a lot to be nervous about. I'm on a bus heading to who knows where and I'm surrounded by strangers with issues. I just don't know why I'm here."

"You don't, huh?" Harvey said. "Well as my dad used to say, 'When the duck flies south, join him.'"

Diana shot Harvey a perplexed look. "What the heck does that mean?"

Harvey chuckled and answered, "I haven't the slightest. His sayings never made a bit of sense to anybody."

Becoming more serious, he continued, "But anyways, you say that you shouldn't be here and yet you are. Why did you come?"

Diana didn't know how to answer that. She looked back out the window, trying to find some way to explain it. But how could she? She didn't understand why she was sitting here either. The city had been left behind miles ago and now beautiful green rolling hills were all that she could see. A small herd of horses grazed, seemingly unaware of the intrusion into their peaceful world, as the large yellow school bus roared by.

"I don't know. I honestly have no idea. I wish I could give you an answer."

She turned to him, "Why are you here, sir?"

"Call me Harvey," he corrected her. "And I'm here because I felt I should be. That's the best answer I can give. My life got turned upside down a few months ago, and I needed something new, something exciting. Otherwise, I would have gone mad."

"What happened?" Diana asked.

He smiled, "I don't want to talk about it. But let's just say, I had nothing left afterward. When I received the phone call, I thought it was just a joke. But something inside told me it was more than that. After the invitation came in the mail, I knew I had to come and find out what it was all about. Was there only an invitation in your envelope?"

"No," she answered. "It contained an old photo of my father when I was just a baby. I guess I came for the same reason you did. I just knew I had to."

She barely finished her sentence when she suddenly felt so exhausted that she could barely keep her eyes open. Diana stayed awake just long enough to see Harvey lean against the seat in front of them and fall fast asleep. Her world suddenly grew dark.

—

The hotel owner smiled as he placed golden nameplates on the doors to each room. He couldn't wait for his guests to arrive. He had sent Chester to retrieve the guests in the exact location that his invitations had read. The people he had chosen for this special occasion had been on his mind for a long time. He couldn't wait to introduce himself to them. As he slid the last nameplate into place, he heard the squealing sound of well-used brakes.

—

The jarring of the bus coming to a complete stop woke Diana from her deep sleep. She rubbed her eyes, trying to regain clear vision. She heard Charles yawn, just waking up also. Harvey was already standing and taking a long stretch, running his hands along the ceiling of the bus.

When she could focus again, Diana gazed intently out her window. It was a heavily wooded area, much like the area she grew up in. When she was young, she'd loved to play among the firs and the pine trees, pretending that she was the ruler over all the animals and wildlife or that she was an animal herself, living in the dark forest.

Up the rocky path about twenty yards away stood a giant building. She had never seen anything like it. The entire structure was made out of huge gray stones stacked one on top of the other. The only things that separated the stones were great glass windows seeming to beg somebody to enter. The building was too tall to see what the roof was made of, but she could only assume it was as solid as the rest.

Chester stood and smiled at the groggy and confused group.

"Well here we are folks," he chirped. "Welcome to the Jasper Hotel."

Chapter 3

"Beautiful!" the young music teacher said and clapped.

The girl blushed and thanked him. She had practiced all week on the song and was so happy that she was able to perform it well for him on her flute.

"You really liked it, Mr. Landon?"

"Courtney, it was marvelous. I can't believe you're only in the sixth grade. Your tone is as pure as a professional!"

She laughed and shook her head.

"Yeah right," was all she could say.

"Now," he continued, "what are you going to practice this week?"

"I am going to practice my chromatic scale and choose a song for the regional music festival."

"That's right!"

Looking at the clock, he patted her knee.

"It looks like our time is up, Cort. You have done very well today."

Standing up, she shyly smiled again. "Thank you."

Before she could walk away, he stopped her.

"Hey, Courtney, you mind giving me a small kiss good-bye?"

She stood frozen, not knowing what to say.

"I know it seems weird, but boys and girls do it all the time. It's really no big deal."

He flashed the smile that she had grown to love so much.

"I don't know, Mr. Landon."

"Come here, dear. It's really okay."

Reluctantly, she walked toward him.

—

Nobody moved. They all stared at the building. Diana didn't know exactly what she had been expecting, but it most definitely wasn't this. The place looked dark and mysterious, even abandoned. There seemed to be no life inside or around it.

"Jasper Hotel," whispered Madison.

"Looks like the Rock Hotel to me," chimed in Harvey. "There is no jasper in this place."

"Follow me, everybody," commanded Chester. "I think dinner should be ready by now. We don't want to keep my Lord waiting."

"Who is this Lord?" questioned Diana, finally finding her voice again. "You haven't said anything about him yet."

Chester smiled. "Well, Diana, it's not my place to tell you. I think he wants to tell you himself. I'm simply his messenger sent to retrieve those he has invited."

Grabbing the large lever beside him, Chester opened the door and stood. He motioned with his hand toward the rest of the group as a gesture to exit the vehicle. Louis slowly stood and painfully walked down the three steps to the soft dirt floor of the large yard that surrounded the hotel.

Courtney, obviously frightened, pressed against the window by her seat, slowly shaking her head, while Charles stormed toward the door.

"It's about time to find out what all is going on here. This better not turn out to be a huge waste of time!"

And with that, Charles joined Louis outside. Harvey followed Charles but was quickly stopped by Chester's arm.

"Sorry, sir, but the master specifically told me to not allow any of you to bring anything of your own inside. You are to come as you are. You will have to leave the briefcase on the bus."

"I will do no such thing!" retorted Harvey.

The friendly man who was just chatting with Diana became an angry and defensive monster, like Jekyll and Hyde. He squeezed the brown case against his chest and jerked away from the driver. His once-kind eyes suddenly squinted and glared with rage.

Chester very calmly held his position and again demanded, "I promise, your possessions will be very safe here, but you cannot bring anything into that hotel. It's part of the deal. You either leave it here or you will be denied entrance. And my dear sir, I am certain that you want to go through those doors. This gift is far more valuable than anything you could have in that case."

Harvey's body relaxed but still he didn't let go of his prize possession. This scene reminded Diana of the day she dropped off John for his first day of kindergarten. Jim and she had both pleaded with him to leave his beloved baby blanket with them before going in. He held it close, shaking his head and crying huge crocodile tears. He was past the age of carrying it wherever he went, but whenever a time came when he was really nervous or scared, the security blanket was back in his tiny hands.

It had broken her heart to take it away from him that day, but it had been for the best. He was growing up, and with age came the painful process of maturing. As it had turned out, John loved his teacher, Ms. Klein, and couldn't wait to go back the next day. The blanket was quickly forgotten. Her baby, John, had become a fearless six-year-old.

Harvey, on the other hand, was still clutching his briefcase while Chester reasoned with him in a low voice. Very slowly and cautiously, he finally handed over his treasured briefcase. Chester cradled it very gently, as if it was a stick of dynamite that could explode at any time. With great care, he placed it behind his driver's seat and stood up again with a huge smile across his face. Harvey took one last look at his security blanket and walked out the door.

Of the other six adults, Harvey was the one Diana slightly trusted. His decision to leave the bus gave her the courage she needed to exit the automobile. She felt as if she was wearing cement shoes as each step took almost all of her strength. She passed Madison, who watched her move toward the door. Courtney was staring at the floor, frozen in place.

The air smelled crisp, as if rain had just drenched the area. She looked around to try to understand where she was, but nothing seemed familiar. Behind the hotel loomed a large peaked mountain. Clouds hid most of its top, and the part she could see was covered in trees. It was breathtaking. Diana felt so small standing there looking up at the towering wall of trees.

The sound of footsteps made her spin around as she saw Madison, still holding tightly to baby Fern, being helped down the stairs by Chester. She obviously had to leave her stroller on board. Diana peered through a bus window trying to see if Courtney was going to leave the vehicle. She knew that Courtney would not be allowed to take her guitar with her and was sure that she would most likely refuse to come rather than to give up her relinquished instrument.

But surprisingly, out walked Courtney, stone faced and empty-handed. Chester closed the bus and clapped his hands excitedly.

"You have all made a good decision today. I know you have lots of questions, as you should, but I promise they will be answered in his time. You just need to find it inside yourselves to trust him."

"Trust needs to be earned," Charles declared. "Isn't that right?"

Chester let out a chuckle and winked, "You are right, my friend. But I believe that when you understand who you are dealing with inside that building, you'll realize that he has earned it."

Quickly turning around, he headed for the hotel and shouted out to the group, "Now that's enough chitchat! I need to get you inside so you can get ready for your first meal."

They all followed hesitantly, not sure of what was going to happen to them after they entered. Diana's mind was racing with questions. Who was this master of the hotel? What was the gift that was promised to her? Where was she? And what was for dinner? The rumbling in her stomach reminded her that breakfast was the only meal she had eaten that day. Louis expressed amusement as she placed her hand on her talking stomach.

"It would seem you are as hungry as I am!"

She faked a smile. "Yeah, I think I might be."

Diana heard the jingling sound of keys from Chester, who was at the front door fitting a large golden key into the keyhole just under the door handle. Before her were two enormous double doors standing between her and hopefully many answers to her bewildering questions. The entrance was one you would see on some majestic royal castle, oversized and unnecessarily cumbersome.

Chester turned the key, and leaning against the two doors, pushed them open with great force. They creaked very loudly as they parted and gave way to an extremely large passageway into the great hotel. They stepped into what Diana guessed must be the main lobby area minus the front desk. Dozens of black leather sofas were grouped in sets of three facing each other. Large scenic paintings covered the vast walls. She gazed intently at a particular one of a local bar with motorcycles parked in front of it and a man leaning against the wall smoking a cigarette.

That's an odd painting, she thought to herself.

She turned to see what else was in the spacious front room. A big-screened television hung on the east wall in front of two rows of black leather recliners. On the south wall roared a fireplace. Its dancing flames were warming up the large area in front of it.

The group paced the lobby, each in awe of its beautiful tile floors, spacious ceiling boasting four overhead fans, and five clear grand windows dressed elegantly with purple velvet drapes. They stopped, facing a round clock mounted directly above the fireplace.

Madison pointed out what they were all thinking. "That clock doesn't have numbers! And that second hand is moving way too fast!"

Diana had noticed the same thing. There were the hour, minute, and second hand as one would see on any other clock face, but the second hand was moving twice as fast as it should be. The hour and minute hand showed that it was about 3:45, but there were no numbers or other symbols signifying the exact time.

Madison continued, "That's the oddest clock I've ever seen."

And just as quickly as they were dazed by the numberless time keeper, they were snapped back into reality by Chester's obnoxious clapping. The sudden thunderous noise caused Diana to spin around and bump into Madison.

"Careful, lady!" Madison chided. "I'm carrying a baby here, or are you blind as well as clumsy?"

"Back off, Madison," Louis jumped in. "It was an accident."

Madison took a deep breath and hugged her baby tighter. Diana gave a small smile toward the homeless man and mouthed the words, "Thank you." He just nodded and gave her a friendly wink.

"You will get your tour gradually as your visit lengthens, but now it's time to go to your rooms to freshen up," said an impatient Chester.

"Rooms?" questioned Charles. "Listen, I am not spending the night here! I have to get back home. My family is going to wonder where I am."

"Charles, just relax. You're family is fine, and you need to be here. Now, there will be no more discussion. Follow me."

The group looked at each other quizzically and walked toward a door located across the room. It was not nearly as massive as the front door and they all walked through one at a time, not knowing what to expect. Charles was the last one to move, and when he finally did, he grumbled the whole way. Diana couldn't understand what he was mumbling but did pick out a few choice words.

The draft that hit her in the face as she walked through the door carried with it a tantalizing aroma of something cooking in the oven. Her mouth immediately started to water, and her stomach rumbled again, even louder this time. Louis immediately left the group and started heading for the elegantly ordained table that was set before them. Courtney looked around and followed after him.

Chester laughed and beckoned. "Yeah, that's for you, but not quite yet. Come follow me first."

He directed them to a spiral staircase located to their right as they entered the room. Chester took the railing, climbed a few steps, and then looked back at the assembly bunched together again. With his head, he motioned for all of them to keep pace.

In a single-file line, they marched up the stairs to the rooms that Chester had referred to. When they had all reached the top, Chester peered back down the stairs and chuckled. Diana followed his gaze and saw Louis, still standing at the bottom staring up toward the rest of the group.

"You coming?" yelled down Harvey. "You apparently can't eat until you visit your room!"

The group snickered, but Louis just looked down at his feet. He looked back up the flight of steps.

"There is no way I can climb up those stairs," he replied. "My knee is throbbing as we speak. Is there an elevator?"

Chester walked back down the stairs. "All you need to do is sit on the railing."

Louis shot an extremely confused look his way. "Excuse me?"

Repeating himself and patting the railing, Chester commanded, "Sit."

Favoring his right leg, Louis stepped on to the bottom stair and pulled himself up onto the banister. Immediately Louis started sliding up the railing. With the ease of an eight-year-old gliding down his grandparents' banister, Louis defied gravity and in his seated position, found himself with the rest of the group at the top. He sat stunned, stiff as a board. Chester ran back up the steps and took his arm, helping him back to his feet. Diana and the rest of the group stood wide-eyed and speechless.

Chester grinned. "The master doesn't discriminate."

Pointing down a long narrow hallway, he smiled. "Here we are, your rooms."

Not one of the invited guests looked. It seemed nobody even heard Chester. Harvey was busy investigating the mysterious stairway as Diana held the arm of the near-fainting Louis. Charles and Courtney were whispering quietly together, darting suspicious eyes between the cheerful tour guide and the magic staircase. Madison stared at nowhere in particular, deep in thought as Fern played with her hair, oblivious to the strange occurrences around her.

—

The hotel owner stood shadowlike in the distance, watching his invited guests grow more and more confused and agitated. He knew Chester could easily handle the situation, but his appearance would need to be made soon. Each person, he knew, was not ready yet to receive the gift. He hoped that every single one would leave with it, however. It would be dangerous for them to go back home having not received it.

—

After repeating himself three times, Chester finally regained the attention of the distracted group. He led them down the hallway, pointing out each individual's rooms. Diana noticed the brilliant gold plate mounted on each door listing the soon-to-be occupant.

Chester read each nameplate as he passed them, "Madison Sooner, Courtney Koontz, Charles Hartford, Diana Newman, Harvey Moore, and Louis Simpson."

After reaching the end of the six doors, he turned and looked over the group. They had each stopped at their designated room, staring back toward Chester and waiting for the next instruction.

Chester, waving a hand, commanded, "Enter your rooms and get ready for dinner!"

"It's locked!" shouted Charles, jiggling his doorknob. "Are you going to give us some keys?"

Chester answered, "The door is locked only to those who don't belong inside. If the door recognizes you, then you may enter. There is a small microphone in the wall to the left of each room. All you have to do is speak into it and it will open."

Louis spoke into his microphone, and grabbing for the doorknob, face-planted into a still-locked door.

"Oh yeah," continued their tour guide. "It will only work if you say the password."

Rubbing his nose, Louis shot back, "That would have been nice to know!"

"So what's the password?" inquired Diana.

Chester started to walk away down the narrow hall and spoke over his shoulder, "Everyone's is different. You must speak into the microphone your greatest fear. Dinner's in fifteen minutes."

And with that, Chester disappeared down the long, narrow way.

—

Various fears swept through Diana's mind as she tried to pull out her deepest one. She glanced behind her and saw Charles standing very still staring at his microphone probably trying to discover his. Louis had already spoken quietly and entered his room. The slamming of his door caused Fern to start whining a bit. Madison, ignoring her baby, leaned in to speak. Seeing Diana looking around, she glared at her, not wanting to be overheard. Diana swung her head back around to face her door just as she heard Harvey enter and close his.

She tried desperately to come up with the right response as Madison entered her room.

"Wait!" Charles suddenly shouted, causing Diana to jump once again. "How do these people know what our fears are? First they know where we live, they know our names, and now they know this! I don't trust them at all."

Courtney looked up at him with red eyes and mascara-streaked cheeks. She nodded in agreement.

"I want out of here," she barely spoke.

Diana walked over to her and embraced her. The young woman accepted the hug, and Diana could hear her sniveling against her shoulder.

"It's going to be okay," said Diana, not believing it herself. "Just get ready for dinner. I think eating would be a good first step in getting all of this figured out."

"Yeah," agreed Courtney, wiping her eyes and sniffing. "I agree."

The knot in Diana's throat grew as she walked back toward her locked door. Her fear was clear in her mind, but to actually say it out loud was too painful. After taking a deep breath, she spoke the dreaded words. She immediately tried the doorknob, and the door easily swung open. Before entering, she looked back at the red-headed musician, and she was opening her door as well. Charles had already disappeared inside his room.

—

So many things caught her eye at once that it was too overwhelming to take it all in. It was a fairly small room, about the size of an average hotel room. She grinned as her eye caught sight of the bed directly in front of her, its headboard nestled against the back wall, the bed itself positioned directly in the center of the room. She rushed toward it, plopped down on the edge, and instantaneously was sucked into the middle. It was a water bed with a Bugs Bunny and Friends comforter, matching pillowcases, and a nice long red body pillow resting in the center. It was her bed, the one she had dreamed of since she was little girl. She laid down, resting her hands behind her head, and enjoyed the gentle waves passing to and fro under her body.

On the left wall looming over her was a giant mounted head of an Asian elephant. On her right, looking directly at its animal counterpart, was a mounted head of a roaring lion. She stood on the edge of the bed and ran her fingers through his coarse mane. She felt his sharp teeth and shuddered at the thought of coming across one of these gigantic beasts in the wild. These were all things she loved as a child.

Kara would love this room, she thought.

Hopping off the bed, she noticed the end table next to the bed housing three framed photos. She knelt down, taking the closest one in her hands. It was the last professional family photo taken before they'd separated. She was wearing a purple tube top and tan pants, sitting down in front of a kneeling Jim wearing the same shade of purple button-up shirt and black pants. John was kneeling sideways to their left and was dressed in a clean white polo shirt and khaki slacks. Diana found herself quietly laughing as she remembered the ridiculous argument they'd had before leaving the house about what color he would wear. She finally agreed to white after many refusals on his part to wear purple.

John looked so handsome though in the picture—his beautiful blue eyes staring directly into the lens and his muscular cheekbones that created a gorgeous smile. He had been the crush of many girls in his class. In junior high, he would always blush and deny any of it when Diana would tease him about all the hearts he was breaking. She knew he was just going through an anti-mother stage now, and she longed for the day when she could sit down and have a good conversation with him again.

Kara knelt on the other side of her parents, resting a hand on Diana's shoulder. Her beautiful lavender dress was tucked neatly underneath her knees. She suddenly needed her little girl, to feel her wrap her tiny arms around her neck, and whisper, "I love you, Mommy." They used to spend hours just talking about girl things, ranging from Barbie to the latest fashion, while Diana ran a brush through Kara's long, shining black hair. She always wore it long, never wanting it to be cut.

This photo used to be her life. She wanted so badly for that to be a reality again. Lisa kept reassuring her that there was hope, but as the months passed, the hope evaporated quickly like one's breath in winter.

Her eyes skidded over to another framed photo behind the first one directly to the right. It was another family photo, but this was one in which Diana was the child. She remembered the major disagreement that this picture caused between her mother and father. The church had been creating a member directory that included photos of each family. Her father had wanted no part in it, but because of the constant nagging and prodding by her mother, he had finally relented. And this was the resulting capture of the Potton Trio—a man dressed in dirty overalls, very straight-faced, his lovely, smiling wife in a pink blouse and black skirt, and their daughter, dressed in a bright red and white shirt and black leggings, wearing more of an irritated look than a smile.

That had been her childhood as she remembered it. This photo portrayed the first eighteen years of her life to perfection. She didn't know who the owner of this hotel was, but she started liking him less and less. Why did he have to frame this photo and place it by her bed? The last thing she ever wanted to do was dredge up her past. She had come for rest, not this.

The last frame was on the left side of the table even farther back than the other two. It didn't hold a photo, though. It simply possessed a white piece of paper with one word typed boldly in the middle: *me.*

Confused, she left it untouched and searched the rest of the room for whatever else this mysterious stranger might have left for her. Directly across the room from her bed was a closet full of women's clothing. A note hung on the door that read: "Put on the yellow dress."

She thumbed through the shirts, slacks, skirts, and blouses until she found a bright lemon-colored dress hanging, ready to be worn. She took it by the hanger and laid it carefully on the bed. It was absolutely stunning. It had lace edging on each sleeve and on the bottom. A sash was sown in the middle of the back to be used as a belt. Turning back to the closet, she got on her knees and looked at the assortment of shoes sitting nicely in two rows. On the end rested a beautiful pair of heels in the same shade of yellow as the dress. She pulled them out and sat them at the end of the bed, along with her chosen attire.

She then headed through the doorway immediately to the left of the closet and walked into a small tiled bathroom. Directly in front of her was a sink with an arched faucet and the hot and cold handles on each side. An oval-shaped mirror was hanging on the wall just above the porcelain sink. The toilet was adjacent to the sink, followed by the bathtub and shower. Dark green towels hung lifelessly on the towel rack behind her. For being such a magnificent hotel, she expected a better-quality bathroom, but she couldn't complain too much. At least she had her own.

She washed her face, trying to understand the past few hours of her life. Although the dress was very elegant, the note commanding her to wear it made her uneasy. But did she dare not wear it to dinner? She changed into the yellow outfit.

Suddenly Chester's voice came booming into the room through a speaker in the corner above the door. "Dinner is ready. Please come now!"

Diana took one last look at her reflection in the mirror and headed for the door. She reached for the handle but stopped. Turning around, she picked up the jeans she'd been wearing and removed the photo of her dad from the front pocket. Walking over to the nightstand, she placed the picture into the frame covering her family's church directory photo. Turning, she headed to the door, turned the handle, and walked out.

Chapter 4

Diana pictured herself as a cartoon character hovering above the earth and floating on a scent trail toward something delectable and mouth-watering. Her belly once again reminded her of how little she had eaten that day. She had no idea what time it was because sometime between the bus and her room, her cell phone had turned off and wouldn't turn back on again.

She carefully took each step down the spiral staircase while balancing uneasily on the yellow heels. Louis's voice echoed up from the dining room. Diana could hear him chatting away about how amazing the meal looked. When she reached the bottom, she could see that she was the last to arrive. There they all were around the table: Charles, Courtney, Harvey, Louis, and Madison with baby Fern on her lap. An empty chair rested on the left side of Charles and another on the left side of Harvey.

Diana walked to Charles's left and pulled the chair back. He quickly put his hand down on the chair and shook his head.

"We all have assigned seats, Diana. Yours is over there."

All the others nodded in agreement. She found her place to the right of Courtney; her name was clearly printed on a place card positioned perfectly in the center of her plate.

After sitting, her gaze wandered from person to person, each in a bright new outfit. All the women were wearing dresses in the exact same style as hers and the men wore fancy suits with vests, ties, and jackets. Charles was decked out in red, Courtney was in orange, Harvey green, blue adorned Louis, and Madison was dazzling in indigo. Like a painter's pallet, Diana's yellow was the last color to be added.

The sparkling china that had been set in front of her was like none that she had ever seen before. The glasses, bowls, and plates were made of what seemed to be crystal but were so clear that they were nearly invisible. A brown, well-cooked turkey steaming in the middle of the table tempted her taste buds. There were other dishes filled with potatoes, beans, and fresh green salad. The white tablecloth disappeared underneath the feast. They all sat wondering whether or not to begin.

Breaking the silence, Charles yelled to nobody in particular, "Hey, can we eat yet!"

Silence.

"This is ridiculous," stated Madison. "Chester rushes us to dinner like we are gonna be late or something and then leaves us sitting here while the food gets cold."

Fern started whining as if on cue.

Silence.

Louis appeared to be under a lot of stress not being able to eat this feast displayed in front of him. He was like a small puppy told to sit while eyeing the tantalizing bone waved in front of him teasingly. He finally cracked.

"I'm eating! I don't know about you guys. I can't wait any ..."

His impatient words were sharply cut off by the sound of footsteps coming from the lobby. All eyes were glued to the swinging door as they anxiously waited for whoever was coming to walk through. Diana found herself cracking her knuckles. Everything in her wanted it to be friendly and happy Chester, but inside she knew it wasn't. They all had been anticipating the meeting of the owner, but now that the time was upon her, she dreaded it.

The creaking of the door made every guest tense up, and eyes strained in the direction of the incoming man. It slowly opened, and Diana held her breath.

—

The tan Toyota truck swerved in and out of traffic recklessly. Louis gripped the steering wheel and made the sharp left turn into the parking lot. His head grazed the ceiling of the cab as he raced over the large speed bump. He parked in his usual spot and ran toward the back door of the shop.

As he grabbed his time card, a voice hollered from behind him.

"Simpson!"

He turned around and saw the red-faced man leaning against the back of a rusty Honda. "Simpson, this is the fifth time this month that you have been late. I've been gracious for a long time now, but this is the last straw."

"Sir, I can explain …" Louis started.

The man interrupted by storming over to him and leaning in, smelling his breath.

"That's what I thought!" he growled. "You have a serious problem, Simpson. Until you get that under control, you are going to always be a loser. I can't have people like you working in my establishment. You are too high risk. I'm sorry, but you're fired."

"Sir, please," Louis begged. "I need this job …"

"Get out!"

—

No sound could be heard in the room as a short, middle-aged man walked in clothed in a violet suit, the same style as the other men were wearing. He took quick strides across the room, scanning his guests as he headed for the last empty chair. Standing behind the chair and holding on to its back, he smiled.

"Welcome everyone. I hope you find the accommodations hospitable. I'm glad to see everyone's wearing their specified outfit."

He nodded as if very proud of himself. "I must say that you all look ravishing!"

That voice! Diana recognized it as the man that called her on the phone. This was Lisa's mysterious friend.

"We look like we are in the circus," complained Charles.

Laughter erupted from the unknown man. He patted Charles on the shoulder several times.

"Well, I promise there will be no circus here. Trust me. Everything here is for a reason."

Turning to the rest of the group, he continued, "Please begin eating. I do hope you enjoy."

Louis didn't miss another beat. He immediately stood and started carving the turkey. Madison dished herself some of the mashed potatoes and began passing the dishes to the left. Diana sat motionless, not finding the motivation to begin. She looked back up to the man, still standing and smiling softly to the brightly colored crowd. His eyes were so kind. Diana lost herself in them until he turned and met her gaze.

"You may eat, Diana," he said to her while outstretching his right arm over the table. "Eat all that you want."

She grabbed the bowl of green beans next to her, dished some onto her plate, and quickly handed it off to Courtney, who seemed as hesitant as she was. Diana should have been deathly afraid being among so many strangers and eating a meal prepared by somebody so mysterious. But the presence of the new arrival only made the atmosphere calmer and more peaceful. Charles's countenance even relaxed, and he started filling his plate with turkey and salad as well.

The man sat down and joined in the circular passing of the food. Small conversations started at various parts of the table as they all began eating. Louis and Harvey laughed and chatted with each other to the right of Diana as they both seemed to inhale helping after helping. Charles and Courtney positioned themselves awkwardly around each other after he realized that she was left handed. This brought a slight chuckle from the man and also Madison as she watched. Diana was shocked, not realizing that Madison could smile. Seeing her laugh brought even more ease to Diana's mind.

The rest of the meal was uneventful. Every stomach was becoming filled as the dishes were emptied. After some time, the guests of the round table sat back and moaned and groaned. Diana's stomach, no longer growling from starvation, now ached from over consumption.

"That was delicious," Louis said, forcing the words out between satisfied moans.

The man smiled. "I'm glad you enjoyed it, Louis."

He lowered his napkin after wiping his mouth and folded his hands on the table.

"Now, all of you are probably wondering what this is about. I can assure you that it is no joke. You are not being scammed. The calls I made to you were very serious. I chose each of you to be here, and I'm ecstatic that you came."

"So, you're the one who called me on a pay phone, huh?" questioned Louis.

He looked directly into the bearded man's eyes and grinned.

"I am."

"What is this gift?" asked Charles, continuing the inquisition.

"I can't tell you at this time. You will have to figure it out for yourself."

"Oh great," mumbled Madison, frowning. "Are we on some sort of reality show or something? Why does it have to be a mystery? Just tell us what it is. We've waited long enough."

The owner became more serious. "You haven't waited as long as I have, Madison. And to answer your questions, you are not on a TV show, and I can't tell you because you wouldn't believe me even if I did."

Charles turned to face him directly. "What is your name? You seem to know all of ours."

"That will have to wait as well, Charles. I'm sorry, I know it doesn't seem fair, but you will have to trust me. My name is far too wonderful for you to understand."

Charles frowned at that response and began to snap back with another question.

"What do you—"

"Charles," the man interrupted. "Please, just accept that answer for now. You will understand later."

Diana finally found the courage to speak up and ask a question.

"How do you know so much about me, sir?" she inquired, her voice trembling a bit. "My room was prepared for me in ways that nobody should have known. How do you know?"

"Don't let that scare you, Diana," he answered in a gentle voice. "I know you better than you know yourself."

Sitting up abruptly, Charles pointed at each person, "The rainbow! All of our clothes! We are sitting in order of the colors of the rainbow!"

Patting Charles on the back, the man beamed. "Nice observation, Charles." Quickly standing, he threw his napkin onto his food-stained plate. "Please, will you all join me in the lobby?"

"Why the rainbow?" asked Harvey after they all found a seat among the couches.

"Because they are important to me," he answered.

"Why are they important to you?" questioned Charles. "Looking for a pot of gold or something?"

A burst of laughter erupted from Diana. It wasn't so much that the comment was funny, but it was more that Charles had made a joke.

Maybe he just needed some food in his stomach to lighten him up a bit, she thought.

The owner laughed too.

Fern started squirming frantically in Madison's arms. She whined and desperately made an effort to free herself from the arms of her mother. Madison finally gave in and laid the baby on the floor. Liberated, she kicked hysterically and giggled.

Louis smiled and leaned over, wiggling his fingers to entertain the child. The baby cooed and reached for his hands. Diana could tell that Madison was on edge, keeping an eye on Louis like a mother bear protecting her family. The room was quiet except for Louis and the little one making noises back and forth.

"About this gift," the hotel owner said, breaking the silence, "we should discuss it more. It is the reason you are here."

"And for rest," Diana spoke up.

"Yes," smiled the stranger, "and for rest."

He continued, "My greatest desire is to see each of you receive the gift, but it will be completely up to you. As we spend more time together and have further conversations, I think that it will be clearer what is going on. I again want to assure you that this is no trick. The time you spend here will change your life—if you let it."

"If anything, I'm receiving free room and board," stated Louis matter-of-factly. Looking at the owner, he tilted his head. "It is free, isn't it?"

"Yes, it's free," the man said and nodded.

"I've never stayed anywhere free before," muttered the homeless man. "Well, if you don't count that religious shelter that I eat at every week. I don't count it because they make me listen to a sermon. I hate sermons."

"Me too," piped up Courtney. "All they want to do is make you feel guilty and then take your money."

Charles laughed and nodded excitedly. "That is exactly how I feel too! I went a couple of times just to see if this God thing was for me. I received a few handshakes, some aches in my back from the wooden pew I sat in, a guilt trip …"

"And a partridge in a pear tree," Courtney said and giggled, finishing his sentence.

"Yes!" agreed Charles. "You should rewrite that song!"

"I went to church," Madison spoke up.

Tears welled in her eyes, and she looked down at her baby, now very still. Fern lay on her back, head tilted to the side with her hand resting against Madison's foot.

"What happened?" asked Diana.

"Nothing," she murmured. "I hate church too."

Diana looked at the hotel owner, who listened intently to every word each of them said. He didn't seem as cheerful as he was a few minutes ago but instead sat there stone-faced.

"What about you?" Louis said, looking across to Diana. "Have you ever gone to church?"

Diana nodded and pulled her feet up underneath her.

"I used to go every Sunday as a kid with my mom. I didn't pay much attention to what was going on. Drawing is usually how I made it through each sermon."

"My wife was the churchgoer," piped in Harvey. "I accompanied her on major holidays, but the church was definitely her thing."

He paused a moment and continued, "And that worked for us. I didn't need it, but for some reason she loved it. She would meet with a bunch of women from there every week and talk about who knows what. I've always said, everybody needs something, and for some it's a hope that there is a God somewhere out there that takes care of us. I had my work, my wife, and the beautiful game of golf."

He chuckled and looked at the hotel owner, who was listening to his every word. "What do you think, stranger? You think that we are watched over by some deity?"

The owner sat motionless. Everybody looked at him, waiting for his response.

He put his chin in his hands and looked up directly at his inquisitor.

"I know we are."

With that he stood up and headed for the door to the dining room.

Looking over his shoulder, he called out to his guests, "You should all head to bed. It has been a long day, and I can't promise that tomorrow will be any shorter. You will be awakened by the sound of trumpets. Please get to breakfast as fast as you can. I'll see you in the morning."

"Wait!" shouted Charles after the owner. "What time is it anyway? There's no clock in this place and my watch stopped."

Diana shot a look to the red-suited man. She thought of her cell phone that was also no longer working. This place was getting stranger the longer she stayed.

The hotel owner stopped at the door and looked back. "That's because when you are here, there is no time."

Chapter 5

The handsome young man stared at the sleeping infant in his arms. He very gently caressed the soft skin of her arm, and he couldn't hold back a tear. He leaned over slowly and every so slightly touched his lips to the baby's tender face. She smelled so good to him.

Suddenly, something diverted the father's attention, and the baby began to gradually rise upward, out of his arms. The man, unaware of what was happening to his child, stood and walked away. The baby rose and headed toward the heavens. The wailing of the infant became distant as she disappeared into the clouds.

—

Diana sat up sweating. It was only a dream. She ran her soaked palms through her hair, trying to recover from her nightmare. She turned on the lamp next to her bed and squinted as her eyes adjusted to the sudden intrusion of light. When her vision cleared, she quickly eyed the frame on the nightstand. Her father was still there holding her in the blanket.

Even though her thoughts regrouped, fear still knotted her stomach. She couldn't understand the dream no matter how hard she tried. It seemed so real, although she appeared to be only watching from a distance, watching her being held by her father and then floating out of sight.

She headed to the bathroom hoping to shake the horrible nightmare. She stood in front of the sink searching for a glass. Her mouth was so dry. Realizing there was no cup, she resolved to go to the kitchen to find one.

The thought of leaving her bedroom frightened her even though her room had proven to be just as unnerving.

She crept down the dimly lit hallway toward the spiral staircase. Not quite knowing where she was going, she grabbed the handrail and slowly took each step, descending to the lower level. She assumed the kitchen was behind a door at the end of the dining hall that she had seen earlier. Deep inside, she knew that a glass of water was not the real reason that she had left her room. Her dream was haunting her, and she was trying to escape.

When John or Kara were young and had run to her in the middle of the night with a nightmare, she was always the strong and courageous one, assuring the kids that it was not real and even checking in their closets and under the bed to make sure the monsters were gone. At this moment, she was the weak and scared little girl. And unfortunately, she had nobody to run to.

Taking the last step, she headed straight toward the mystery door. Diana didn't care what was behind it. She just wanted to find out more about this place. There were too many unanswered questions, and if she couldn't sleep, she might as well research.

"What are you doing?"

The voice from the table made Diana's heart sink into her toes. A gasp of breath escaped from her throat as she fought back a scream. Her eyes directed themselves over to where the voice had come from. Sitting at the table was Madison. There was little light in the room but enough to recognize her dark, long hair and pale skin. A shawl was draped over her front; it cradled a nursing Fern.

Joining her, Diana sat at the table across from the young mother.

"I couldn't sleep," she told her. "My curiosity got the best of me and I wanted to look around more. I want to find out more about this place."

Madison nodded. "I can't sleep either, and Fern doesn't sleep well away from home. She was hungry and I decided to feed her down here. The room they gave me here gives me the creeps. It's," she paused, "well, it's too me. There's no other way to say it."

"I know what you mean," agreed Diana. "My room is set up in a way that nobody should know how to."

Madison stared at nothing in particular, but Diana could almost see the wheels moving in her mind.

"What are you thinking?"

Madison met her eyes and shrugged.

"I don't know what to think. I'm not even sure why I came. Can I ask you something?"

"Of course."

"I decided to accept this invitation to an unknown place from an unknown person and I brought my baby with me. Does that make me a bad mother?"

Diana arose from her chair and circled around to the other side of the table. She sat directly next to Madison and placed her hand on the mother's arm.

"Forgetting your child in a rest area on a road trip and not realizing it for three miles makes a bad mother."

Smiling, Diana continued, "And I should know."

Madison laughed out loud. "Oh, I'm sure you're a wonderful mother. How many kids do you have?"

"Two beautiful children," Diana boasted. "John is fifteen and a freshman in high school. Kara is eleven and in fifth grade."

Madison grinned. "And which one was lucky enough to spend some time alone in the bathroom?"

"John," Diana said, snickering. "Poor kid was crying by the time we got back. A nice woman was trying to calm him down by offering him some M&Ms. He doesn't remember but we have told him and now he won't let me forget it."

Madison was smiling. "My parents forgot me at my grandparents' house once. It wasn't traumatizing at all though because they spoiled me while my parents were gone. They said they forgot me, but I think they did it on purpose to get some alone time."

"How long did they forget you?"

"Two days."

They both burst out laughing, trying to muffle their voices with their hands. Madison picked up Fern and leaned her over her shoulder and lightly patted her on the back. This was the most at ease Diana had felt since leaving her house to go to the corner. But something was bugging her.

"I don't want to bring down the conversation," Diana leaned forward, "but can I ask a question?"

"Shoot," said Madison.

"I really needed to laugh, but to be honest I never thought it would come with you. I remember you on the bus snapping at Louis just trying to make conversation. What was wrong?"

Fern burped and Madison wiped her baby's mouth with the rag on her shoulder. She then held the baby in her arms and cradled her.

Looking up, she answered, "I was really nervous. I didn't know who anybody was or what their motives were. I was feeling very guilty for bringing Fern with me, and I guess I was being overprotective of her. I suppose I should probably apologize to him tomorrow."

Diana nodded, "That's very understandable. We were all on edge at that time. Louis seems very kind. I'm sure he will forgive you."

"So," continued Madison, "am I or am I not a good mother?"

Diana smiled. "The fact that you are concerned about your baby in this place and what kind of a mother you are shows me that you are doing excellent. A good mother isn't perfect. As long as you put Fern first at all times, you are an amazing parent."

Madison looked down at her child, "I love you, kiddo."

Looking up, she continued talking to Diana.

"Not to change the subject, but what do you think of our host?"

Diana had lain in bed after everybody went to their rooms and thought about that very subject. He was so baffling. His comments about knowing her more than she knew herself scared her tremendously. There were many things in her life that she hoped nobody would ever find out.

But no matter how weird he seemed, she felt calm around him. She remembered his facial expressions as they talked in the lobby. His eyes remained gentle as he listened attentively. She couldn't read his eyes very well to know what he was thinking. All she knew was that he was interested in each person there.

And he was direct with his words; everything seemed to have purpose. He had invited everybody here for a reason. In his words, he'd chosen them. And his answer to Harvey's question about a God that watched over people. He answered with such certainty.

"I'm not sure what to think yet," answered Diana, pulling her feet up underneath her on the chair. "I want to trust him, but I don't know enough about him yet."

"I like him," Madison said quickly.

Diana looked up surprised.

"Why is that?"

Madison shrugged. "I'm not really sure. There's just an aura about him that is pleasant. His voice, words, and actions are all so loving and gentle. It seems he really does care about us. The only thing that makes me leery of him is my room. He knows way too much."

"You spoke my thoughts exactly," said Diana. "What's in your room that bothers you, or is that too personal?"

"Some of it is too personal. My college diploma is framed and on the wall. Family pictures are on the nightstand. And my bed is exactly the same one I had when I was a little girl. I don't mind all of that. It's the other things I hate."

"The only thing I couldn't stand in my room was a family picture that was taken for some church phone book or something. I covered it up with a picture I had in my pocket."

"You were able to sneak in something, huh?" asked Madison with a wink. "I thought for sure he would make me leave Fern. Chester was pretty strict about leaving everything on the bus."

Diana laughed. "I guess I did sneak it in. But it was given to me in my invitation I received from the hotel owner. So I guess it was allowed in."

"What was allowed in?" questioned a deep voice from the stairway.

Both ladies spun around to see who else was in the room. The sleeping baby whined a little as the sudden jerking of her mother almost woke her up. Their eyes watched as Harvey walked over to the table and sat down.

"Couldn't sleep either, ladies?"

They both shook their heads no. Madison was caressing Fern, who had fallen asleep again.

"Well, two out of three of us can't sleep," joked Madison.

"I was sleeping fine," said Diana, "but I had a really weird dream that woke me up. So I got up to investigate more about this place and Madison was here feeding Fern."

Madison smiled, "Yeah, I think I gave her a mild heart attack!"

"Seriously," continued Diana, "if I get scared one more time …"

"What will you do?" inquired Harvey.

Diana just looked at him with a grin of embarrassment.

"I have no idea."

They all laughed.

"Well I can't promise you that you won't get scared again," said Harvey. "This place seems to do that to people. I think we all are a little more on edge than we normally would be."

Madison nodded. "I agree. We were just talking about the hotel owner. What do you think about him?"

Harvey rubbed his mouth with his hands. "Well, I've been doing a lot of thinking during my sleepless night. I think I'm starting to figure him out."

Both women looked at each other with confusion written all over their faces.

"You have?" they both asked.

"Well, maybe a little. I think I know who he is claiming to be. If he is, then we are into something a lot deeper than any one of us could dream. If he's not, then he's a complete nut job or scam artist. We all need to be very careful here."

"Who do you think he is?" Diana questioned, now chewing on her right middle fingernail.

Harvey looked down and shook his head.

"I don't want to say yet just in case I'm wrong. It would sound completely crazy to both of you."

"Trust me, it probably won't shock us too much considering all that has happened so far," stated Madison very seriously.

"I'll tell you tomorrow after I think on it a little longer. I just came down because I heard voices down here. I should probably head back up. The owner says that we will have a long day tomorrow, and my old body can't take long days after short nights."

He patted Diana on the hand and gave them both a smile.

"Don't worry, I'll figure this out. You two are safe with old Harvey here."

Both women smiled back and they watched the old man climb the stairs back toward the rooms.

"He's right," said Madison. "We should go get some sleep. Who knows what tomorrow may hold."

They both arose from the table. Diana's motherly instinct kicked in and she leaned over and gave Madison a hug. She accepted it, and they smiled as they both turned toward the spiral staircase.

"I'll see you in the morning," Diana said softly.

"Goodnight," sighed Madison.

Chapter 6

"An empty chair at the dining room table, a faraway son doing all he is able. Fighting for freedom and longing for home, but the idea of peace makes him feel sooo alone ..."

The song floated into Diana's room from next door. She rolled over, tilting her head up off her pillow and listening to the beautiful voice coming from Courtney's room. She strummed softly and sang a very sad song but with a voice of an angel. Diana sat up completely, closed her eyes, and focused intently on the melody floating in the air around her.

She almost fell out of bed as an obnoxious trumpet blared through her loudspeaker. Anger set in as she realized that was their alarm clock. She had no idea how long she had slept, but she felt more rested than she had been in many months.

"I guess I've found rest here already," she said aloud.

After showering, brushing her hair and teeth, and choosing an outfit consisting of a light blue blouse and faded jeans, she headed out the door to breakfast. She met Courtney in the hall.

"That was a pretty song you were singing earlier," she complimented Courtney.

"Thank you. The owner here was at least generous enough to give me a guitar in my room. It's a song I've been working on for a few weeks. It is almost done."

"I would love to hear more of your work sometime."

"Well, I've thrown all my others away. This is my first one I've written since ..."

Courtney lowered her head and started walking away.

"I don't really feel like talking about it. We should go to breakfast."

"They can wait," Diana said, trying to calm her. "I think you need to talk about it."

Courtney looked up, brow furrowed.

"Listen, lady, thank you for the compliment about my music, but I really don't feel like talking, okay? We should go join the others and eat!"

Diana backed up a couple of steps and raised her hands, a defeated foe waving a white flag in surrender.

"I didn't mean to get nosy, dear," she said, trying to make amends. "I just know that when I talk about what is bothering me, it makes me feel a lot better."

"Fine!" yelled Courtney, "You really want to know? I quit high school, tried to make it big with my band, they ditched me, and I'm left with nothing. That about sums it up."

Diana slowly walked toward her, cracking her knuckles. The sudden outburst shook her, and she tried to think fast on her feet. She wanted to settle Courtney without causing a scene. She regretted prying into her history.

"I'm sorry, Courtney. I guess I was just hoping I could help. You're right. We should just go to breakfast."

Courtney's face was unreadable. Diana reached a hand toward the girl's hand. She didn't pull away but allowed Diana to hold it.

"Are you okay?"

Courtney nodded and looked up with the saddest eyes that Diana could ever remember seeing.

"I'm sorry too, Diana," Courtney almost whispered. "I've never liked people getting into my business. Sorry for snapping."

"No harm done," she replied with a smile.

Pointing toward the stairs, she released her hand. "Shall we?"

—

The table was decorated with scrambled eggs, piles of bacon, sausage, and ham on several different glass plates, stacks of toast made with all kinds of bread, round bowls overflowing with apples, oranges, peaches, and bananas, and pitchers of orange and apple juice and milk. Every guest except Harvey was sitting anxiously waiting to indulge in this smorgasbord. It seemed to Diana that the atmosphere of the group had changed dramatically from the night before. They seemed cheerful and pleased to be there. She figured they must be just as rested as she.

"Where's Harvey?" asked the owner, walking into the room.

They all shrugged.

"Haven't seen him," said Charles.

"Can we start without him?" questioned a hungry Louis.

The hotel owner laughed. "Yes, please do."

They all dug into the beautiful meal set before them. Almost immediately, Courtney was biting into a peach and Louis had dumped a huge amount of eggs on his plate while already munching on a strip of bacon. Charles was guzzling a glass of whole milk, Madison was buttering a piece of wheat toast, and Diana was cutting into a piece of steaming ham. The owner took his place next to Madison and smiled as he watched the group chow down.

"I know who you are claiming to be!" boomed a deep voice from the stairs. *"I think I figured you out!"*

Every head spun with great alarm to the man walking down the stairs. The owner stood and motioned for Harvey to sit.

"You have? Who do you think I am?"

Harvey sat down and piled some eggs on his plate and grabbed two pieces of white toast. Everybody had stopped eating and stared as he filled his crystal plate with all the delicacies that they had already started devouring. They waited for his reply.

Once he got what he wanted, he looked up and stared at the owner.

"Well, you know us better than we do. You also love rainbows, know for a fact that there is a God, you claim that your name is too wonderful for us to understand, and you live outside of time."

As he talked he raised a finger for each point on his list. Diana leaned on his every word, forgetting about the savory aroma of breakfast and wondering what point he was going to reach.

He continued, "I am knowledgeable enough about church to know that this can only describe one person. And if you are claiming to be this person, I'm out of here because you're crazy!"

The owner's attention was fixed on Harvey. His plate was still empty and his elbows were on the table; his chin rested in his hand.

"Okay, that's fair, Harvey. But who do you say that I am?"

Harvey reclined against the back of his chair and crossed his arms.

"You are claiming to be God."

Diana's mouth dropped open. She couldn't believe what he had just implied. Silence flooded the room as every eye in the place turned to the hotel owner. He never changed expression but only nodded.

"So, if I agree to your charge, you are walking out the door. Is that right?"

Harvey didn't move but continued to stare at the mysterious man.

Not waiting long for a response, the man continued, "I suppose that is going to be up to you. I want all of you to finish eating and think about what he just proposed. We will discuss this after breakfast."

The atmosphere died down drastically. Each person ate in silence, looking around awkwardly between bites. Diana couldn't understand what had just happened. Was the hotel owner claiming to be God or was he just playing along with Harvey's theory? The thought haunted her and yet simultaneously intrigued her.

—

The hotel owner sat in a recliner praying for those up in their rooms getting ready for the day. He faced a black screen on the television while holding the remote in his hands.

"Father, no matter how this plays out today, I pray that they won't leave. Keep them here and allow them to hear what I have to say."

—

Diana had brushed her teeth and now sat on her bed thinking about breakfast. Could the hotel owner be God? Is there a God? Her mom had prayed to him all the time and she'd died a lonely housewife. She heard all about him, the loving and gracious Lord of lords.

Jim had wanted nothing to do with church or his mother-in-law's faith, and that was not a battle that Diana had found worth fighting in her family. They were married and had two beautiful children and were living the good American life without the help of God. But then the affair shook her world, and God didn't help that either.

Anger filled her again thinking about her life as it was. John and Kara were her saviors and the reason she got up in the morning. Her job brought her no joy, and her love was now stripped from her.

There can't be a God, thought Diana. *Who is this guy really?*

She walked out of her room and nearly ran into Charles.

"What do you think?" he asked without even looking at her.

"I think he's a kook," answered Diana.

"My thoughts exactly. I am going to find out what this is about. The longer I'm here, the more nervous I get. I feel this is some kind of trap or something."

Diana nodded. "We are going to be on some news show sometime. The missing six from North and Sixth."

Diana moved her hand across the air, mimicking a headline. Charles didn't speak another word as they climbed down the stairs and walked through the door leading into the lobby. Madison, with Fern, was sitting in one of the recliners next to the hotel owner. Courtney was standing off by herself staring out the window with her arms crossed in front of her. Louis was kneeling in front of the fire and was pushing logs around with the fire poker. Harvey had not yet arrived.

"... and I love how her eyes look exactly like yours," spoke the hotel owner to Madison.

"That's what everybody says," replied Madison looking extremely comfortable around the mysterious host.

The man looked up and smiled. "Oh good; we are all here now."

Diana looked behind her and sucked in a deep breath, startled as she realized Harvey was standing with them right behind her.

"Could all of you come find a seat in these recliners?"

Nobody moved for a short moment as they looked at each other nervously, but all eventually walked slowly to the leather chairs. Each took his or her seat and gazed up at the large television set in front of them.

"We gonna watch a movie?" questioned Louis.

"No, they are more like home videos," answered the host. "Your home videos."

"Excuse me?" exclaimed Courtney.

Charles stood up and pointed his finger at the host.

"Listen here, buddy, I've had about enough of you. Tell me the truth right now! Who are you, and how do you know so much about us!?"

"Please sit down, Charles. I know this doesn't make sense to you and you don't like circumstances in which you are out of control. But you need to let me show you all of this. It will make sense after you understand what is going on."

Diana expected Charles to bolt out the door. He had acted extremely uneasy since they were standing on the corner. She was surprised he had lasted this long. She secretly hoped he would leave. He always created tension among the group with his outbursts and childish tantrums.

But he sat back down in his seat at the request of the host. The owner turned to the TV and using the remote, began the video.

Diana leaned forward and started chewing on the skin surrounding her thumbnail. Everybody in the leather recliners tensed as the black screen switched to a young girl in a classroom. Nobody knew what to expect.

"That's me!" shouted Courtney. "How did you get this? This was never recorded!"

"That is true," the host explained. "But you have to realize that everything is laid out in front of me. I see all things at all times."

Nervously, each guest watched a small redhead girl defend another girl being bullied by a mob of high-strung, snobby blondes. Standing between her and the group, she told them to leave the girl alone and go away.

The movie quickly switched to a teenage boy teaching his younger sister an algebraic problem at their kitchen table. Charles sat up stiffly as the scene played out. Diana assumed that the young boy must have been him. Her heart was racing, wondering when she would appear on the television. It wasn't long before a little blue-eyed girl was shown cleaning a very messy kitchen as her mother walked in from outside. Diana remembered the great pride that she had felt when she'd seen the smile on her mother's face. She again felt the joy of being swept up in her arms as her mother hugged her.

Louis laughed and pointed as the scene changed, "Hey, that's me!"

Diana watched a very young and good-looking Louis run to a smoking vehicle that looked as if it had just plowed into a tree. He quickly opened the door and proceeded to pull injured people out of the car while a man with him looked them over and nursed their wounds.

One by one the videos passed in front of their eyes, each star being shown in the midst of heroic and generous acts. Diana viewed Madison slipping an envelope of money into a student's mailbox, Harvey surrounded by gunshots and smoke carrying two bleeding soldiers from the front lines, Charles smiling for cameras holding an award at some science convention, Courtney sitting down with a young girl showing her how to play a guitar, Louis giving another homeless man half of a burger he had found, and her own self hugging a crying Kara and placing a Band-Aid on her daughter's elbow.

Diana had no idea how long they sat there because she sat captivated by the movie. Many of the scenes made them laugh, and some evoked tears. Memories rekindled as they partook in momentous occasions of each other's lives. For the first time since they had met, the six strangers sat together like friends.

When the screen went black, conversations broke out among the guests. They complimented each other and asked for further details about things that they had seen.

Eventually the hotel owner stood up in front of them and raised his hands, asking for silence. The talking died down, and all attention was on the man before them.

"There is a purpose for showing you this."

"I'm sure there is," piped in Charles. "I'm sure there is."

Ignoring the comment, he continued, "I just showed you many events in your life that make you proud. These were all times that you did something good. I trust it made you feel good about yourself."

They all nodded.

"I want to give you a present now."

He passed to each seated person a small gift. Diana held in her hands a square box wrapped in yellow paper with a bright pink bow on top.

"This box represents each of those commendable things that you just watched. They are beautiful, aren't they?"

"This is the prettiest paper I have ever seen," whispered Madison, holding Fern in one hand and her box in the other.

"Can we open them?" asked Harvey, tugging at one end of the blue ribbon on his present.

"Only if you are ready for what's inside," answered the host. "Harvey, that box represents your purple hearts and army ranks. All of your accomplishments and good deeds are symbolized by these attractive gifts."

"Yeah, yeah, yeah," interrupted Charles. "Let's just open them."

The host watched each person closely as they tore open their presents. The women carefully opened theirs so as to not tear the paper. The men ripped into theirs. Diana looked up quickly as Harvey threw his box down in disgust.

"Is this a sick joke!?" he yelled. "You can't be serious?!"

Diana realized what he was complaining about as she opened her box and reached in. Her hand sunk right into a pile of garbage; empty gum wrappers, a banana peel, and numerous crumpled up papers. Quickly pulling out her hand, she groaned loudly.

"Oh gross!" exclaimed Charles. "I can't believe you would make me open up these old worn hankies!"

Madison looked over in disgust.

"That is sick. I thought this oily rag was bad enough."

Courtney didn't say a word as she held a muddy towel.

"Underwear. Old holey underwear. That's my purple hearts, huh? Excuse me but those are worth a lot more than this!" screamed Harvey.

Louis just sat there laughing.

"I guess my good acts are as good as this," he said, holding up a stained burp rag.

"Listen please," the host spoke calmly to the irate group. "I want to explain. None of you realize why you are here. You think you are receiving a gift like this—something gift wrapped. I want you to start thinking deeper than that."

Charles arose from his seat.

"Listen, pal, I've had enough of your games. I want out."

"Just give me a few more moments. Then each of you can choose what you want to do. Please."

Charles sat again but was very stiff, and his forehead was wrinkled as he listened.

"At breakfast, Harvey said that he thought I was claiming to be God. I want to end the mystery of my identity. I am the one they call Jesus."

"Oh great," mumbled Madison.

The whole group shot confused and bewildered looks to each other. Diana sat stunned at this man's claim.

Before anybody could question him, the man continued. "I wanted to show you many good things that you have done to teach you a truth that you may not accept. Only God is good, and without him, nothing you do on your own can be good. They are as valuable as those rags in your boxes. Those obviously weren't the gifts I referred to in the invitation. This was just a lesson."

"Not to cut in," interrupted Courtney, "but if I wanted a lecture I would have just visited my mom."

"Your rags," continued Jesus without acknowledging the comment, "have damned you from the beginning. I love each one of you. When you were in the womb, I remember the joy it was to decide how you were going to look, what your voice would sound like, and to design every intricate part of your being. The only problem is that we don't have a relationship. Some of you deny I exist. And it breaks my heart."

Diana held back a sob as she watched the man fight back tears. Catching his breath, he continued, "That is why I brought you here. If all of you continue your lives the way they are, you will never experience what I planned for you from the beginning. I drew you here by invitation to reveal myself."

Before their eyes, scars appeared. Diana noticed large round ones in his wrists and long, jagged white marks on his forehead. He looked at his own scars and then raised his eyes to the wide-eyed crowd.

"Your rags did this to me, along with your disobedience and constant unbelief. But I suffered anyway because I wanted opportunities like this to offer you something that you can't even imagine."

He paused. Nobody said a word.

"I want to offer you a place in my family. In this family, you will experience life like it was meant to be lived."

"And how does that happen?" questioned Charles.

"Just believe what I'm saying is true. I died for you as a man, but a perfect one. But when I took my last breath, I died a wretched and condemned sinner because your sins came into my life. I died the death that you deserved. There was a moment when I didn't want to go through with it. This death would separate me from my Father and just the thought almost killed me. But if you will only believe me, the eternal life I live will also be yours. You will be perfect like me."

Louis looked puzzled. "If you died, how are you standing here? Are you a ghost?"

"No, Louis, I am not a ghost. Three days after I died, I raised myself from the dead. I am alive and have the power to make you alive as well."

"Are you saying we are not alive?" asked Diana. "We seem to be."

"Physically yes," replied Jesus, "but spiritually, you're as dead as I was hanging lifelessly on that tree. You need to be resurrected internally just as I was physically. And the only way that can happen is if you trust me with your whole being."

The host knelt in front of the confused group.

"Your gift is waiting for you if you will only receive it. Will you?"

Chapter 7

The little boy sat against the wall by the stairwell just out of eyesight from his parents who were seated downstairs on the couch. They never knew that he snuck out of his bedroom most nights and he enjoyed playing the spy. He curled his knees up to his chest and listed to his dad and mom's conversation.

"I can't believe we are having this discussion again, Cheryl! For the last time, we are not going to church."

"I know that's what you have said," she replied nervously. "But the Tanners have asked us over and over again and I think it would be fun to join them."

"It's a waste of time! You know it and I know it. Why subject our child to a bunch of nonsense and superstition? Church is only for the weak ones that need something to get them through life. There is no God! Charles will be intelligent and rely on facts and things we can see. We are not going. Period."

His mother stormed out of the room, stomping up the stairs. Charles quickly darted back to his bedroom just in time. He stared at the glow-in-the-dark stars above his bed.

Closing his eyes, he whispered, "There is no God."

—

Jesus waited for any one of them to respond. He watched his guests grapple with this new idea. Charles and Courtney frowned and grew tense. Harvey was rubbing his hands together so forcefully his knuckles turned white.

Louis calmly regarded his burp rag and chuckled. Nobody answered his question.

Charles stood and walked to the middle of the room and then paced. He would pause and point at him, looking as if he was going to say something, and then turn around and pace again. The others had repositioned themselves to face Charles and began to watch him nervously walk back and forth. He finally spoke.

"You are not God."

His voice sounded angrier than any of them had heard up until then. Sweat appeared on his forehead as he pointed directly at the kneeling host.

"You can't be God. There is no God. I'm sick of your games, lies, and whatever you are trying to pull here. I'm done with this."

With that, he turned and headed toward the door. Jesus stood and extended his hand toward the irate man.

"Charles, please don't go. Give it time. You will understand."

Charles turned back toward the group with flared nostrils and squinty eyes that glared right through the man standing before him.

Pointing at his own chest, he questioned, "I don't understand? *I* don't understand? Now listen to this one thing—I know what is real and I know what is not. God is not real!"

"Do you know everything?" Jesus asked him.

"Of course not! Nobody does."

"Do you know half of everything?" continued the host.

"No! Why are you wasting my time with this pointless inquisition?"

"Let's say you do know half of everything, Charles. Is it possible that God could exist in the half you don't know?"

The question stopped Charles in his tracks. The look on his face revealed many emotions, confusion and anger above all.

"You set me up."

"Did I?"

Jesus walked toward the fuming individual. The group held their breaths, waiting for the showdown to begin. Harvey slowly began to stand. Madison cradled her baby close to her chest.

"May I take you on a short walk, Charles? I think it would be beneficial for all of us. We need to talk alone."

"I don't think there's anything to talk about," retorted Charles.

"Please join me," continued Jesus. "If after the walk you are still angry at me, I will call Chester and he will drive you home. I promise."

Charles darted a glance toward the rest of the group, who were still watching intently. Harvey had taken a couple of steps toward the two men. He seemed to be waiting for a brawl to begin and was ready to jump in and break it up.

Looking back, Charles nodded. "Okay."

"Good." Jesus smiled. "Come with me."

The two walked toward the fireplace and stopped before a painting hanging to the left of the hearth. A beautiful array of colors erupted on the canvas to form a peaceful forest scene. Fresh green pines surrounded a swift brook with large, peaked mountains towering in the backdrop.

Charles looked confused as he glanced between the painting and the brown-haired man.

"I thought we were going to have a private conversation?" he asked. "Everyone can still see us."

Jesus patted Charles on the shoulder.

"I know. I need you to close your eyes."

"Excuse me? Close my eyes?"

"Please do," Jesus commanded softly. "Then we can go for our walk."

Reluctantly, Charles closed his eyes. Jesus turned to the group and smiled.

"We'll be back soon. You can do whatever you want until we get back."

The group looked at each other quizzically.

Turning back to Charles he said, "Okay, here we go."

—

A breeze suddenly brushed the skin of Charles's face. He opened his eyes and almost fell backward, startled by his surroundings. Pine trees stood all around him and before him swept a stream over many perfectly round rocks. A deer walked into the opening, gazed at the two men, and walked along, unfazed by the sudden visitors. They were standing in the painting.

"Who ... how di ... where are ..."

"Don't try to understand this," Jesus said with a grin. "Just enjoy the beauty."

And beautiful it was. The sun was glaring down on the forest from the west. A chipmunk ran by, stopping only inches from Charles's foot. It looked up at him, chirped, and darted toward the nearest tree.

"Where are we?" asked Charles, finally finding his voice.

"It doesn't matter really," answered his host. "This could be anywhere in the world. The same point would be proven."

"What point is that?"

Immediately a deafening roar of beating wings made him lift his hands over his head for protection. Hundreds of birds flew above them and landed in the trees. Every branch was lined with a great number of them. Large amounts of water fowl landed on the banks of the stream.

"This point," yelled Jesus over the flapping wings.

Charles waited until all the birds had landed. He recognized many different kinds from his biology courses; blue jays, red-breasted robins, crows, finches, mallards, and even others that he had never seen before. All of the feathered creatures were singing their hearts out.

"What point are you trying to make with these birds?"

Jesus gazed at the vast choir that surrounded them. Charles watched him close his eyes, lean his head back, and smile. His scars were again invisible.

"What are you doing? Are you going to answer my question?"

Jesus opened his eyes and looked at Charles, his smile fading.

"What do you think these birds are singing about, Charles?"

"Singing about?" he asked, taken aback by the question. "It could be for a wide variety of reasons. They sing when the seasons change or they are trying to communicate with the other birds. Some may be trying to attract a mate or defend their territory. That would be my guess."

"They do communicate that way. But what about all the times you see one bird sitting alone on a branch singing his heart out like all of these are doing now? What are they singing for?

Charles became flustered.

"I don't know. Nobody can. We can only guess. Why are you asking me this?"

Jesus looked at him with a sparkle in his eye.

"I'm asking because I know the answer."

Turning toward the mysterious host, Charles leaned in. "Do you mean you know the answer to why the bird sings? How can you know that?

Jesus looked at the birds still belting out their tunes.

"Because I understand them. I know their language."

Charles shook his head trying to comprehend what this man was saying. So many questions came to his mind, but only one found its way to his lips.

"Huh?"

"Charles, I know the words of the birds."

He shook his head again.

"You know what they are saying? That's insane. Can you prove this to me?"

Jesus grabbed Charles's hand and again closed his eyes.

"Sure," he answered. "Allow me to show you what I hear."

The sound of the unified voices dropped Charles to his knees. He listened to the song of the birds. It was greater than any choir he had ever heard,

Holy, holy, holy is the Lord God Almighty, who was and is and is to come. Holy, holy, holy is He, our Creator who provides and cares for each one. Holy, holy, holy is the Lord God Almighty.

Charles looked up at Jesus, who basked in the sound of the feathered ensemble. He listened in amazement. The beautiful song left him paralyzed. And just as soon as it had started it quickly reverted back to simple chirps. And as if on cue, they all took flight, a vibrant, multicolored canvas against the reddening of the sunset.

Standing, Charles barely found his voice. "That song was from the birds?"

Jesus grinned and nodded. "Well, not just the birds. The trees, water, and rocks joined as well.

Charles's mind was racing. He couldn't explain what he had just seen and heard, but it still didn't convince him.

"That was amazing," Charles whispered. Looking to Jesus, he continued, "Did you show me this to prove that there is a God?"

"I am glorified in my creation. The stars, plants, and animals all point to me. I created them by speaking. You see, I am love, and I wanted to have others to show my love to. By nature, I seek relationships. But when it came to you, Charles, and the rest of mankind, I spent more time on you. I formed you with my hands and gave you a spirit. This is something the rest of creation can't claim. I made you in my image; a created being with a spirit can have closer fellowship with me than any other thing I have made, for I am Spirit. But you want to know the ironic thing about it all, Charles?"

Charles didn't answer, and Jesus continued.

"My creation that I love the most is the only one that hates me. They disown me so much they convince themselves that I don't exist. These birds sing more to me than those I chose to die for."

All that could be heard was the rushing of the creek working hard to smooth out the rocks it swept over. Charles avoided eye contact with the man who was claiming to be his Creator. Then a thought made him smirk.

"Jesus, if that's who you really are, if you are so perfect and loving, how can you be so prideful that you demand worship from everything else? Isn't that hypocritical?"

Jesus paused a moment and knelt by the stream running his hand through the brisk water. He sat on a nearby rock and dried his hand on his pants.

Looking up at his guest, he explained, "I created people with a natural tendency to worship. Everybody worships something. What do you worship, Charles?"

Charles could only shrug.

"Many have chosen to worship money and possessions, but all it does is create more greed and frustration. Some have worshipped people, whether they are leaders or family members, but humans have a sinful nature and will sooner or later disappoint. Most worship themselves, and that only leads to broken relationships and grief. Charles, those who choose to worship me are the only ones who find true fulfillment and peace. I am forever faithful and true. I want the best for every person, and I have the power to give it. But if you want to choose to find satisfaction in something else, it doesn't matter what I can do for you. Does it?"

He didn't have an answer. Everything this man said made sense, and yet it only fueled his anger. Charles leaned against a tree and folded his arms.

"Are we done with our walk?"

Jesus stood and smiled. "You want us to be, huh? Well I wanted to show you something else."

He walked over and took hold of his arm.

"Close your eyes, Charles."

Too exasperated to argue, Charles complied. The sound of the brook disappeared and immediately it was deafeningly quiet. His body felt unnatural. He opened his eyes and wanted to scream but only a wince could be heard from him.

Charles was looking directly at the earth floating in empty space. He quickly looked for Jesus, who was still beside him floating as well. Tears formed in his eyes as fear rushed through him like he'd never felt fear before.

"Are we really in space? Where are we really? What is going on? I don't like this!"

The words came faster than he could think. Panic seized him, and he grabbed the arm of Jesus and squeezed as hard as he could.

"Settle down, Charles," Jesus said calmly. "You will be okay."

"Okay!" he shot back. "Okay? How am I okay? I'm floating in outer space. How am I breathing?"

Jesus started laughing. "Charles, you are with me. I promise that it will be okay. I just wanted to bring you here since this is your area of expertise."

Charles's heart sank, and he glared at the grinning man next to him.

"Oh, so you just brought me here to mock me, is that right? Okay, you created this! It's beautiful! Now take me back. I want to go home!"

As if he hadn't heard him, Jesus continued.

"Didn't you win an award for your thesis on the development of planetary evolution?"

"Yes I did," Charles answered smugly.

"I thought I would bring you out here to see for yourself. Look at your world. Isn't it beautiful?"

The fear that had gripped Charles was subsiding, and the beauty of earth dazzled him. He had studied it for so long but had only seen pictures. They had done it no justice.

"It's fantastic."

His eyes were glued to the blue planet reflecting the light from the sun.

"Do you know how fast the earth travels around the sun?"

Charles knew this question easily. Since he had a master's degree in astronomy, this line of questioning was his cup of tea.

"Sure I do. It's between 66 and 67 thousand miles per hour."

"Have you ever wondered how it stays on course?" Jesus asked, continuing his inquisition.

"It's gravity. The sun keeps us in its gravitational pull just like the moon stays in earth's. But the inertia of the earth repels it at the same time so the balance keeps the earth on track."

Jesus nodded as if in agreement.

"But have you ever wondered how it really works? As you know, if the sun pulled the earth any closer, then it would be too warm for life, and if it pulled away any farther, then it would be too cold."

Charles nodded in agreement.

"Yeah, it's mind-boggling."

"Do you ever find yourself scared about the earth going off course? There are so many factors that have to remain exactly the same."

"Yes. There was a point in my life during my studies that I became frightened. Somehow for the millions of years of the earth's existence it has stayed on course, but if any factor does change, it is the end. I just don't think about that possibility."

"What if," Jesus continued, "you didn't have to worry?"

Charles looked up, confused.

"What do you mean?"

Jesus held his hands out toward the earth. "What if there was a God holding everything together and making sure it all stays on course? Then there wouldn't be any need to worry."

"That is true. I guess if someone wants to believe that sort of thing and give themselves some kind of hope, then that is good for them. I'm a realist."

Jesus laughed.

"That's what I want to show you, Charles. There is more out there than you know. You may be a realist in the context of your knowledge, but there's a completely different realm of life that you are not aware of. I know you want to know truth. I don't doubt that for a minute. But unfortunately, you can't know truth apart from me. I am the Creator of all things, all of this you are seeing now. I hold it in my hands and keep it running so that you can live. You may not believe it, but what you think doesn't make it any less true."

Charles had no response. His heart was racing again. He hated this man and yet at the same time, was drawn to him. His desire was to be home with his wife and kids, and yet the wisdom of this man glued him to his words. He couldn't decide whether he wanted to go or to stay.

"Are you ready to head back to the hotel, Charles?"

He could only nod.

"When we return, are you going to stay or leave?"

Charles looked up at the man who was gazing at all the celestial bodies. He did look like a proud painter admiring his work of art hanging on display in some museum.

"I will stay for a while longer. I'm not sure what to think yet."

Jesus smiled. "Take all the time you need."

Chapter 8

Diana and the rest of the group sat speechless as they watched the two men disappear right before their eyes.

"Charles?" Madison cried in a gasp that was barely audible.

Harvey walked over to where the men had just been standing a moment ago. He searched the area looking for any sign of them.

Diana joined him. She knelt down and looked in the fireplace. They were gone.

Harvey peered into the picture of the wooded area that Jesus had pointed out to Charles.

"Do you think they went into the picture?" he asked.

A laugh erupted from Courtney.

"Do you mean like on *Mary Poppins?*"

"Something like that I guess." he answered very seriously.

Diana looked at the painting and ran her hand across it. It was a beautiful scene, and she wondered who had painted it. Madison walked out of the room carrying her baby and mumbled something about Fern being hungry.

"Are you okay?" Diana called after Madison.

She turned around just before passing through the door.

"All of this is making me nervous. I'd feel better taking my daughter to the safety of my bedroom."

And with that she pushed through the door and disappeared behind it.

Louis left his seat and admired some of the other artwork that covered the main room walls.

"There are sure a lot of paintings," he said to nobody in particular.

Diana couldn't have agreed more. It seemed there was no need for wallpaper. Whatever space there had been was covered with a picture or a window. The sun blared through as she marveled at the vastness of it all.

Harvey had moved on from the forest painting and was studying a picture near the front door. Louis was working his way down the line of images while favoring his knee with a noticeable limp. Diana noticed that her little finger didn't have much of a nail left; she had been nibbling it since the disappearance.

"I've seen this bar before," Louis declared, pointing to the painting that Diana had noticed when she'd first entered the hotel. "I have no idea who the man with the cigarette is, though."

Diana walked over next to Louis, who limped to a couch and sat down. She once again looked at the picture but now even more closely.

"You know this place?" she asked, pointing to it.

"Sure do," said Louis, rubbing his sore knee. "Wish I didn't though."

"What happened there?"

"Well," he started, "that's the first place I—"

His sentence was interrupted by the sudden reappearances of Charles and the host. Everybody turned, stunned by the intrusion.

Jesus looked at Charles. "Are you going to stay?"

Charles looked different to Diana. He seemed calmer and much more somber. His complexion was much whiter though.

"Uh, yeah, I guess," he stammered, "at least for a while longer."

He seemed lost for words. This wasn't like him at all. Diana didn't know what had happened or where they had gone, but something had impacted Charles.

"Great!" exclaimed Jesus as he walked toward the door. "I'll see all of you in ten minutes. Lunch will then be served."

After he left, they all watched as Charles sat down on one of the leather couches and leaned back, staring at one of the ceiling fans.

"Are you okay?" questioned Courtney coming over and sitting beside him. "You don't look so good."

Charles didn't even acknowledge her presence. Diana could tell his mind was far away and they would have to wait to find out what had happened.

Harvey tried as well, "Charles, where did he take you? What happened?"

As if he couldn't hear, he sat stone faced, not moving a muscle. The rest of the group stayed motionless as well, waiting for him to answer. The awkward silence was too much for Diana.

Turning back to Louis, she asked, "What was that place in the painting you were talking about?"

He looked toward her, taking his eyes off of Charles for the first time since he had arrived back from his walk with Jesus.

"It's the first place I ever tasted whiskey. I was twelve years old. I followed my dad one day to see where he was going. He was always gone and I missed him something terrible. His buddies and he laughed when I walked in unaware of where I was. Yep, they gave me whiskey until I couldn't walk anymore."

He looked up. A large tear ran down his cheek.

"Yeah, nice guys, huh? But like any boy, I wanted to be like my dad. I thought all real men drank alcohol. So by seventeen, I was an alcoholic."

Diana's stomach turned over, and she thought she was going to be sick. She couldn't find words. She just sat beside him and held his hand. That's all she could do as the man sobbed.

She looked up and met Harvey's eyes. He shrugged, obviously at a loss as to what anybody could do to remedy the situation. Courtney sat next to the man in shock, talking softly to him. Diana held Louis's hand as he trembled. Diana looked around the room at the four strangers huddled on the couches. This group of strangers was at each other's throats a short time ago, but now they seemed to care about one another. Diana hoped that they could continue getting along. She wasn't sure if she was safe here if she had to rely only on herself.

Bursting through the door, Jesus walked in with Madison close behind.

"It is time to eat if everybody is ready!"

Diana's head jerked up. She wondered if this host could be any more insensitive to the situation. He had to have noticed that things were not going well in the room.

"We may need a minute," said Harvey.

Jesus walked up to Charles and knelt in front of him.

"Charles."

His head lifted off the couch and his eyes focused.

"Charles, it's time to eat. You need some food. I know your mind is full of questions and is overwhelmed with things, but you need to eat. I don't expect for you to understand it all. These were just a few things that I needed to show you. I hope you didn't mind."

Charles shook his head. "I didn't mind although I am not sure I am ready to believe you yet."

Jesus smiled. "And that is fine. Just keep pondering it though."

He stood then, knelt again, this time in front of Louis, who was staring at the floor with bloodshot eyes.

"Louis, you too need to eat. I want to have a talk with you after lunch. Is that okay?"

Louis nodded. "I didn't mean to make a scene. But that picture brings back horrible memories."

Looking over his shoulder toward the bar painting, Jesus grabbed his hand that Diana had been holding only minutes before.

"I know it does, Louis. I brought you here so you could face it head on and defeat what has defeated you for years. If you will allow me, I want to give you a new life."

Louis nodded. "I need a good fixing, Jesus, although my life seems to be way beyond fixing."

Jesus grinned and stood.

"Louis, you haven't started your life yet. Now, everybody, let's go enjoy a good meal. I think we all could use it."

—

Lunch was fairly uneventful. Random small talk filled the air. Diana discussed motherhood with Madison. Fern had already eaten in their room and was now sleeping in a baby carrier on the floor by her chair.

Charles ate silently, listening to the conversations but never putting in his two cents' worth.

Courtney was more talkative than usual, discussing classic rock with Harvey, who seemed to be a huge fan as well. Louis picked a seat right next to Jesus and was silent for the most part. Every few minutes he would remind Jesus of their upcoming conversation date. Jesus, very patiently, repeated that he remembered.

When everybody had finished, Jesus excused them to their rooms. He wanted each person to rest a while and then he would call them back down. Diana could only guess it was another one of his plans to get into their heads. She had been scared of him ever since Charles had returned. The once arrogant and loud man had become a very somber and quiet person.

—

She went into her bathroom to brush her teeth and wash her face.

Looking into the mirror, she frowned. "What happened to you, Charles? What happened?"

The mystery behind the disappearance was haunting her. Charles came back a totally different man. She almost missed the boisterous person he used to be. She was afraid that her time was coming to be alone with Jesus and was terrified about where he would take her and what he would do. She needed to know what had happened.

—

Knocking on Charles's door, she breathed deeply, hoping he wouldn't mind the intrusion. He cracked open the door and peered out.

"What do you want?" he asked, sounding more tired than rude.

"Can we talk?" she requested. "I need to know what happened to you. I'm afraid he will talk to me next, and I want to know what to expect."

Charles just shook his head.

"You will never be prepared for what could happen. I wouldn't have believed it if I hadn't been there."

She looked him in the eyes and begged.

"Please Charles. May I come in?"

The door opened. Her eyes scanned the area, which was arranged similarly to her room. His bed was a queen size and decked out in Mighty Mouse comforter and pillow cases. Diplomas and awards inside very expensive frames lined the right wall. On the opposite wall, in cheaper frames, were many various photos of what seemed to be Charles with family and friends. The carpet was green with white lines across it. She noticed that it was a football field. The backboard of the bed was in the shape of a goal post.

Charles is a football fan? she wondered. She would never have guessed.

"There's nowhere to sit," stated Charles, continuing to stand himself.

"That's fine. I really don't intend to stay long. I just couldn't rest not knowing what happened to you. It seems to have affected you tremendously."

"You won't believe me even if I tell you."

She nodded. "I'll believe you. After everything we've seen and heard here, I'll believe you."

He closed his eyes for a moment and sighed.

"That man who calls himself Jesus showed me things I never should have seen."

He told her everything. Diana found herself sitting down on the edge of his bed, unable to stand any longer. A deepening lump formed in her throat as she listened to Charles's story.

"And so I told him I would stay for a while longer, and he told me that I should just continue pondering what I have seen."

"Have you?" she asked.

"All the time."

She put her face in her hands and tried to breathe deeply.

"Have you decided anything?"

He looked at her with glazed eyes and sat next to her on the bed. Staring straight ahead, he paused.

"I know he isn't like any person I've ever known. Although fear was racing through me, I felt a sense of calm with him. He spoke words that gripped my heart. That's the only way I can explain it. Although what he told me contradicted everything I ever stood for and knew to be real, I wanted to believe him. I haven't decided anything. I don't know what to think, to be honest."

"Do you want to go home?"

He paused again.

"Yes, but no. I worry about my family. I'm sure they are worried sick about me and wonder where I am. But I need to talk to him again. I would hate to admit this, but maybe what I've believed and have been teaching for many years is wrong. He could be telling the truth."

Diana stood and walked part way to the door.

Turning to him she whispered, "If he is lying, we are in serious trouble."

Chapter 9

As the group left the table, Jesus put his hand on Louis's arm and shook his head. Louis smiled and remained in his seat. He watched the rest of the guests climb the winding stairs, chatting amongst themselves as they went.

"How are you going to fix me?" asked Louis.

Jesus laughed. "I don't think it's that simple, my friend. You can be fixed if you want to be. But you have to trust me."

Louis nodded. "Okay. How is this going to happen?"

Jesus rose from his seat and began heading toward the door to the main room. Louis followed him slowly. Jesus stopped in front of the painting that had caused Louis to break down earlier.

"We need to start here."

Louis nodded slowly but kept his eyes on the floor.

"I just need to show you some things so that you will completely understand what I need you to do. Now, if you will, Louis, please close your eyes."

He obeyed and a sudden whiff of cigarette smoke filled his nostrils. He quickly opened his eyes and found himself outside of a building he hadn't seen in over forty years.

The man smoking and leaning against the outside of the bar was seemingly unaware of the two newcomers.

"Can he see us?" asked Louis, trying to come to grips with where he was.

"No," answered Jesus. "We are just observing."

"Why are we here?" questioned a confused Louis. "I know what happened here. I know that it changed my life in a horrible way. Why do we have to visit it again?"

"To fix a problem, we must start at the root. Let's go inside."

Louis felt dread as he walked through the old wooden door leading into his past. Immediately he saw faces that he had nearly forgotten. Louis's father and friends lined the bar laughing, cursing, and raving about different subjects that ranged from women to hunting.

Old man Norris was seated on his regular stool at the far end and nursed a bottle of beer. Any day of the week you could find him there. He was such a regular that even after he died, nobody sat in that stool ever again.

Kurtis, a coworker of Louis's father, annoyed everybody by trying to get somebody to challenge him in a game of billiards. He boasted about being the best there was on the North American continent, but Louis had only ever witnessed him win a handful of games.

Louis's father sat with a half shot of whiskey still in front of him while staring gravely at the chaos. Three young drunks tossed darts at the target hanging on the opposite wall. Bart, Marty, and Louis had been friends since grade school and now worked together at the local supermarket. Almost every evening was spent here talking trash and getting trashed.

Louis admired his young body and full head of dark wavy hair. But standing there with Jesus, he was overcome with embarrassment for his lewd behavior and vulgar language.

"This place was almost home to you for ten years."

Louis nodded.

"Look at your father closely. What do you see?"

Louis gazed at the gray-haired man taking one last swig of alcohol and spinning in his stool to face the rest of the room.

"I see a drunk."

"What else?"

"I see a man who has lost purpose for living. He looks so sad and unfulfilled. It's weird. I never noticed it before until now."

Jesus put his hand around his shoulder.

"He was your hero though, wasn't he?"

"Yes. Everything in me wanted to be like him. He seemed like the perfect model of a real man. All his life he worked hard, was very strong, and didn't take any crap from anybody."

"What do you think now?"

Louis looked at Jesus and back to his younger self, horse playing with his buddies.

"Well, I became him. I guess that's what I wanted."

"And?"

Louis shook his head.

"This place led me down the wrong path. Look at me. I had so much fun here. If only I had known what my future would become. If my mom would have been alive at this time, she probably wouldn't have put up with this, just like my Wanda didn't put up with it either."

"Do you blame her?"

Louis again shook his head.

"All I do is drink. I spend five nights a week at the bar. I'm surprised she stayed with me for as long as she did."

Turning to Jesus, his voice quivered.

"Can I get her back?"

Jesus shook his head.

"That's not for me to say. I will not tell you the future. We are here to fix the present. But this isn't our last stop. I want to make a couple more. Is that okay?"

"If it'll help me, sure."

"Close your eyes."

The next thing Louis saw was the large fluorescent-lit arrow that pointed toward the door of the Two Trails Bar.

Louis forced a laugh.

"Boy, my life sure has a common theme, don't it?"

Jesus ignored the comment.

"You spent hundreds of evenings here didn't you?"

"Yeah. Most evenings were spent here."

Jesus continued, "I brought you here not to remind you of all the nights you got drunk. I brought you here for one specific night."

"Which one?" asked a very intrigued Louis.

"You wouldn't remember it because you never knew what happened. Here you come now."

Louis looked and saw a slightly younger self walking down the dirt road toward the tavern. He wore a blue plaid jacket and jeans with a giant hole in one of the knees. His hair was slightly balding on top, but he was very clean shaven. In one fluid motion, he climbed the front steps and disappeared behind the door.

"What happened this night?" he asked, looking around for something to occur.

Jesus just pointed.

"Look behind that parked white van. Do you see somebody?"

Louis looked hard and when he saw whom Jesus was referring to his stomach turned upside down. He thought he was going to be sick. Out from behind the van, a young boy snuck toward the bar. It was Carson, Louis's oldest son.

The boy carefully tiptoed up the steps, keeping an eye out in all directions. He snuck up to a front window and peered inside, pressing his face against the glass. After a short time, he ran around the side of the building and peered in another window. He stood there for quite awhile watching the action inside.

"What have I done?" whispered Louis. "I've become my father more than I thought. My son is following in my footsteps."

Jesus sent a compassionate look his direction.

"I'm sorry, Louis. But we have to stay a few more minutes. He's not finished yet."

They watched the boy, now bored with spying through the window. He picked up an empty beer can from the ground and pretended to drink it. He stumbled around the parking lot imitating a drunken man. He laughed boisterously and acted like he was yelling at another person, even cursing like he had heard his father do.

Louis started weeping.

"My little boy. What have I done?"

Turning to the man next to him, he pulled on his arm as if he were a child trying to get his father's attention.

"Please, tell me this can be fixed. Tell me that Carson won't become me, a drunken, divorced, homeless man. Tell me he's going to be okay."

"Louis," Jesus answered, "that's going to be totally up to you. You are his role model."

Louis stared at his boy as he regained control of himself.

"We can go now, Louis. One more stop and then we can go back to the hotel."

—

Louis opened his eyes to find himself in his boys' room, Carson lying in one bed and Carter in the other. The last time he had stood in this bedroom seemed like ages ago.

His thoughts were interrupted by a woman walking into the room. It was his beloved Wanda, her beautiful red, curly hair bouncing with every step. She sat on the edge of Carter's bed.

"It's time to sleep now, boys."

"Can we stay up just a few more minutes?" pleaded Carson.

Louis chuckled at how pathetic his son was acting. He remembered many nights where he'd had to send his boys back to bed numerous times. Each time they had a different excuse as to why they were still up. His face sobered as he recalled his anger and uncontrollable temper that he had unleashed on each boy.

"It's already ten o'clock, my dear. Time for lights out."

"Mom," piped in Carter, "is Dad ever going to come back?"

Louis fought back more tears as he watched the scene in front of him.

Wanda ran her hand across the young child's face.

"Probably not. Your dad has made some bad choices, and we can't be with him anymore. I know you don't understand, but it is for the best. We'll be fine, just the three of us."

Carson chimed in, "But Mom, I miss him too. Why can't we be like regular families and have a nice daddy that stays home and plays with us? Why did we have to get a mean one that is never around?"

Louis couldn't hold back tears any longer, and they raced down his face, one after another.

"Now, Carson," chided his mother, "I don't want to ever hear you speak bad things about your father. Nobody is perfect. Even if he has done stupid stuff in his life, he still deserves your respect."

"I'm sorry, Mommy," said Carson, getting out of his bed and hopping onto her lap.

All three smiled and giggled as their group hug became a wrestle match tempered with tickling.

Louis turned to Jesus.

"How do I change?"

"I already told you earlier. Believe in me and you will have eternal life. Trust me with your whole being and you will become a new creation. Your sins will be erased and you will be given a new life."

"Will it fix all my problems?"

"Unfortunately, you will be in the same position you are now and facing the same consequences from your past mistakes. But you will have me guiding you and helping you. I will aid you in defeating your alcoholism and then show your sons what a real man truly looks like."

Louis looked into the eyes of the first man he had ever really trusted.

"I believe you, Jesus."

Smiling, Jesus put both his hands on Louis's shoulders.

"I know you do, son. I know you do."

Chapter 10

A well-groomed young man sat under a tree admiring his sleeping child. He sang a quiet lullaby and rocked her gently in his arms. His eyes glistened as he admired his daughter, whose lips were moving in her sleep, forming a small smile. A slight breeze mussed his hair. The baby shivered as the breeze turned into wind. The father, turning his attention to something in the distance, laid the child in the thick grass, stood quickly, and hurried away.

Shadows began to creep up on the infant, wide awake and crying. A small pack of hungry, gray wolves circled the helpless child. They bared their teeth to emit rumbling growls. The largest of the group leaned down and sniffed the wailing baby, then raised his head and howled.

The wolf flew sideways, somersaulting through the air as a giant paw swiped him away. The rest of the pack attacked, but each one eventually ran away, defeated. The giant body of a lion lay down, encircling the weak and vulnerable girl. The baby stopped crying as the beast lowered its head, and the two drifted off to sleep.

Diana's eyes shot open and stared straight into the open jaws of the lion hanging on the wall above her bed. Her scream was muffled by the pillow as she rolled over and faced the opposite wall. She didn't even realize she had fallen asleep and now was sweating profusely in her bed.

She wondered how long she had been asleep and if anything was going on downstairs. Brushing her hair and teeth quickly and then changing outfits, she rushed down the spiral staircase to find the dining hall empty. She moved quickly through the door into the lobby to see if she could find anybody.

Jesus quickly shifted his gaze from the fire to the woman now standing behind him at the door.

"Hello, Diana," he greeted. "You sure didn't rest for very long. The others are still in their rooms."

"How long did I sleep?" she asked.

"Well that question is all relative," he said, smirking.

"Of course it is," she replied with an over-exaggerated eyeroll.

Jesus resumed his attention to the flames that seemed to dance together to a song that only they could hear.

Diana walked closer until she was standing directly behind the couch on which the man sat.

"About this gift," she started in. "Is it real? Or is this supposed to be some quote 'spiritual journey' for all of us to make? I honestly don't believe you are who you say you are. That just doesn't make sense to ..."

"Louis received his gift," interrupted Jesus.

He spoke as if he was talking to nobody in particular but just relaying a fact. Diana's words were cut short and she stood with her mouth gaping. Jesus glanced back at her, smiled, and stared back at the fire.

"Excuse me?" Diana barely spoke. "Louis has the gift? Where is he?"

"He is upstairs."

"In his room?"

"No, down the hall. He now has access to the rest of the house."

Without another word, Diana turned and ran to the stairs. Tripping over the first step, she made her way to the top. She walked quickly passed the doors to the rest of the hall beyond Louis's room. She never had thought to ask what was down the hall. She just remembered Chester walking down that direction after showing the group to their bedrooms.

Diana took a few more steps and slammed into an invisible wall causing her to stumble backward. Anger flared as her head throbbed from the unexpected hit. She strained her eyes to see what was down the hall but it only ended in darkness.

She turned and began to bang on the doors of every room. Slowly each opened to reveal a very tired occupant annoyed by the rude awakening.

"What is your problem?" Courtney asked rudely.

"Louis is gone," she began. "That man had a conversation with Louis and supposedly somehow Louis accepted the gift. Now he is down that hallway where we can't follow because some invisible wall is blocking us!"

"Whoa, whoa, whoa," Harvey interrupted. "Just slow down, Diana. You aren't making any sense. You need to slow down."

"That's because none of this makes sense!"

"He took the gift, huh?" Charles spoke up, looking only at the floor.

Madison, awkwardly holding Fern with one arm, walked over to the wall and slid her free hand down it. Harvey was doing the same, touching it as if he were a mime performing his act.

"Jesus said that Louis was on the other side?" Madison asked without looking at Diana.

"Don't call him that," whispered Courtney, still motionless by her own room.

"That's what he said," replied Diana. "He said that Louis accepted the gift and now has full access to the house and that he is upstairs down the hall. That's when I ran up here and smacked into this invisible wall."

"Well I suppose we have a few words to speak with our host about," stated Harvey plainly.

—

"What did you do with Louis?" Harvey began the inquisition. "Where is he?"

Jesus, who was now standing by one of the large windows, looked to the confused group.

"I told Diana and she has told you. Why don't you believe her?"

"Diana is not the one I don't trust."

Jesus looked back out the window. "Louis is fine, Harvey. In fact, he's better than he has ever been. He's hoping all of you will join him."

"We would but we aren't allowed down the hall," chimed in Madison.

Jesus smiled. "That is because you aren't family yet. I don't just let anybody have access to my house."

"Family?" they all asked.

"Yes, family," he repeated. "Those who believe in my name for the forgiveness of their sins, my Father adopts into the family. They are made perfect in his eyes because of my goodness. Only the perfect may wander farther down the hallway."

"What if we don't want to go down your stupid hallway?"

Everybody stared at Courtney as she glared at the man gazing out the window.

Without looking toward her, he replied, "Then you must suffer the consequences."

Courtney walked boldly toward Jesus, who now watched her approach.

"Are you threatening me now?" she asked, pointing her finger at him.

"It's not a threat," he said calmly. "It's a promise. I already told you. Your sins have damned you to an eternity apart from me. Without my gift, you are sentenced to eternal death."

"What if that's what I want—to be as far from you as possible?"

Jesus turned back toward the window.

"Then there is nothing I can do for you."

"No, there is something," she bit back. "You can let me go home."

"Home? You want to go home? You mean back to that hotel room?"

She glared at him.

He continued, "And do you miss Robbie? Tell me, is it worth the price he asks to pay for that room of yours?"

Her glare turned to hate as her eyes welled up. Diana could see her body stiffen and her hands ball into tight fists.

"Shut up! Just shut up!" Courtney screamed. "What I do in my private life is none of your business!"

Jesus turned and walked only a few feet from where she was standing. His brown eyes bore into hers. Diana's body now stiffened, suddenly afraid. She didn't trust this man yet, and she had no idea what he was capable of doing.

"Listen, Courtney," he said with anger in his voice, "what you have been doing in your private life nailed my hands to a cross. The day I died, all that you have been doing was placed onto me. Your actions separated me from my Father for three long days. So don't ever tell me it's none of my business."

Courtney took a couple of steps backward and looked at her feet. Diana could feel Madison leaning in toward her.

Jesus, not moving any closer, continued, "And do you really want to move to London with him? I know he has big promises but deep inside, do you really think he is good enough to live up to them?"

Courtney sheepishly answered, "He said there are huge opportunities for me to succeed in Europe. We are planning to fly out tomorrow. He cares about me. He's the only one that has ever really looked after me."

Jesus nodded. "Ah yes, cares for you. Is that what you call it when he slaps you for questioning him? Or how about when he makes you sleep with him even though you don't want to? Is that really caring for you, Courtney?"

Courtney walked to the nearest leather sofa and sat down, placing her head in her hands. Diana could hear her weeping softly. She began to walk toward Courtney to comfort her, but Jesus stopped her with a shake of his head.

"Courtney, I'm not questioning you about all of this to embarrass you. I'm trying to help you figure this out. Robbie doesn't care for you. He only loves himself. You have been taken advantage of by men all of your life. I truly care for you. All of your life you have cursed my name and ignored my cries to you. And yet, I continued to watch over you. And now I have invited you here with me to show you what true life really is. I'm not the enemy, child."

"But what about my music?" she asked, finally catching her breath. "It's all I have."

Jesus sat down beside her.

"Courtney, that's the problem."

Chapter 11

The first part of the meal was silent. No one spoke; neither did anyone even look up. The thick tomato soup was delicious to Diana, but it was the awkwardness between the guests and the host that held her attention. She was generally good at reading people, but Courtney was a mystery. Her aggressive attitude had suddenly been replaced with a very quiet demeanor, and she ate like the rest of them, never looking up from her bowl.

Jesus, slowly sipping his water, regarded each person, his eyes sweeping the table. Everybody avoided eye contact as he scanned the group.

"Why did you come here?" he suddenly asked.

Everyone looked around wondering who the question was for.

"Who?" Diana eventually asked.

"Well, let's start with you," he replied. "Why did you accept the invitation?"

She shrugged, looking at everybody else staring right back at her.

"I wanted rest," she said quickly. "You promised rest and I needed it."

"What kind?"

"What do you mean?"

"I mean what kind of rest. You were getting enough sleep. You even slept in the day you came to the corner. Why would you need rest?"

"I suppose it was more than physical rest I needed. This looked like a good chance to get away from everything. I was hoping ..."

She paused.

"I don't really know what I was expecting. You said you could help me, maybe even change things. I was just hoping for something good to happen. It's been a while."

"Are you disappointed?" he asked.

The question took her aback. The time she had spent here had been so confusing and so much had happened; she'd never really thought about it.

"Let's just say that I've slept well," she finally answered.

"Diana, something good will happen if you let it."

Before she could reply, he turned to the young mother on her left.

"Madison, why did you come?"

Without hesitation she answered, "To receive a gift."

"Really?"

"Sure. That *is* what you promised, wasn't it?"

"It was. But I'm not completely sold on the idea that this was your driving force: to bring your baby to an unknown place to meet a stranger and receive a mysterious gift. Let me ask you again. Why did you decide to come to the corner?"

She grew somber and kissed her baby on top of her head.

Shaking her head, she answered, "I don't know."

"Sure you do. It's okay to talk about it. Just say it."

She took a very deep breath. She turned to the side and met eyes with Diana, who didn't react. Her nature was always to comfort people, but all she could do was look back.

Refocusing on the host, Madison inhaled.

"I guess I'm just searching for the purpose that the man on the phone promised I would find here. Fern is all I live for, which should be enough— but it's not. I've tried education, family, men, and God, and I'm left with nothing. I guess deep down inside, I was hoping that this was my chance to find that purpose. This was my chance."

Jesus nodded. "Thank you for your honesty, Madison. If you just let me reveal some things to you as you stay here, you will find purpose. I promise."

Immediately he continued on to Charles.

"Honestly," he started, "I just wanted to find the joker responsible for the call. There was curiosity about it being a legit invite, but mostly I just wanted to find the person responsible for pranking me."

Harvey spoke when it was his turn, relaying to the group that he had had a very tough year.

"Everything I lived for is now in the past. I needed something to keep me going. I was hoping this would be it."

Jesus now focused his attention on Courtney, who, to Diana, seemed like a meek little girl.

"Would you like to answer the question?" Jesus asked.

She gazed up at him from her bowl. Her eyes had been narrow and angry before, but now they looked at Jesus in a new way. Diana was trying to figure out what she was thinking but was clueless. The words of the host had definitely had an effect on her.

"I was hoping this was my break," Courtney said, interrupting Diana's thoughts. "I'm desperate for my chance, and if this was it, I didn't want to miss it."

Jesus stared back at her as the eyes of each person looked deep into the others.

"This is your chance," he replied. "And it will affect your music. I know you have dreams, but apart from me, dreams are worthless. Even if you achieve them, what do you have left after you die? At best, people will remember your name and your songs. But what about you? Is being separated from God forever worth the shot at short-lived fame?"

"How will your way affect my music?" she asked.

"Believing in me will give your music purpose. Instead of being merely entertaining, the lyrics you write and the music you compose can change lives forever. They can encourage, build up, and give hope. And most importantly, it can please me. And when you leave this place and enter my presence, your true worship will never be forgotten. I remember everything that you do for me."

Courtney looked back at her soup. Diana could almost hear the gears shifting in her head.

"So if I believe in you, you will make me famous?"

Jesus laughed. "That's not a promise, dear. But you will be successful because I will be on your side. And in my book, success isn't judged by profit, CD sales, or music awards. It is based on your heart and why you do what you do. If you sing for my glory, your albums will have an effect and you will live blessed."

"So if I follow you, I can still sing?"

"Oh yes!" Jesus exclaimed. "I love singing! Don't I, Charles?"

Charles just looked at him and nodded.

"What was that about?" asked Harvey, leaning closer to Charles.

"Nothing," he replied.

The redheaded musician continued, "But how would I sing for your glory? What does that mean?"

Jesus smiled. "I think it would be easiest to understand by showing you. Would you like to come with me?"

Nodding, she stood up from her chair to follow him, leaving a half-eaten bowl of soup behind.

"You all are welcome to join if you want," Jesus said to the rest, motioning to follow him.

Without hesitation, each of the invited guests sprung from the table on the heels of their host.

He led them to a picture located between the fireplace and first large window. It boasted a beautiful church with a large steeple snuggled in to what seemed to be a peaceful snowy day.

"Grab hands," he commanded.

As they did, they were transported to that very church and were standing outside its main door.

He turned around to face everybody and raised his hands to speak. Jesus's actions reminded her of a tour guide showing a group of tourists an important building in history.

—

Her mind wandered to Jim on their first vacation as a married couple. They had decided to take a trip hitting some of the major ghost towns in their area so that they not only were spending time together but it was educational as well.

She smirked as she remembered their first tour guide; a very short, middle-aged man sporting a ponytail but very bald on top. He spoke in a nasally sort of tone and a very strong lisp that made him hard to understand.

Jim would whisper jokes about him to Diana, and she would have to turn away and try not to laugh. She slugged him in the arm on the drive back to the hotel because of all of his comments.

But the highlight of the tour was when the guide was speaking about safety through the old buildings.

"You can't be too careful," he explained.

Diana watched in horror as the man tripped over a loose board in the town's old saloon, which sent him sprawling across the room and falling into a young woman who caught him in her arms. His face and head turned a deep red as embarrassment overwhelmed him.

"I lead by example," he remarked.

Diana's stomach knotted as she remembered how happy she was with Jim.

—

"Somebody who places their faith in me is now free to live a life of worship," Jesus began. "A part of that worship is singing. But it's not that easy. I hear things differently than everybody else. Don't I, Charles?"

Again he nodded and again Harvey asked for an explanation.

Charles just shook his head. "I'll explain later if you want."

"Courtney," their host continued, "you asked how one would sing for my glory. Please follow me, and I will show you."

They entered into what seemed like a very traditional service. An old organ bellowed from the corner as the congregants stood with hymnals in hand and followed the direction of the man up front. Each of the five visitors recognized the words to "Amazing Grace" as they echoed through the old building.

"Don't be alarmed," Jesus said aloud. "They can't see us. We are here simply to observe."

Diana noticed the confused and horrified look on Courtney's young face as she listened to the music.

"This is worship?" she asked. "This is what you want me to do with my music?"

Jesus laughed. "I'm not here to show you the style of the music, Courtney, but the heart. Now I want to show you what I hear in this worship service."

Charles leaned over to Harvey. "Hang on, old man. This is when it starts to get crazy."

Immediately the volume of the song was cut in half. They could only hear individual voices now instead of a full choir.

Madison leaned toward a dignified man wearing a pressed white shirt and tie. His brow was furrowed and his chest was puffed out as he appeared to be singing from the depths of his very being. But from the look on Madison's face, Diana could tell that nothing was coming out of his mouth.

Courtney was kneeling beside a very old haggardly looking woman in a wheelchair. She wasn't holding a hymnal, her head was cocked to the side, and her eyes were tightly closed. Her voice was weak, barely audible, but the passion in the way she expressed each word captured each of their attention.

"That is Gladys," Jesus said. "She is a very precious child of mine."

"What's going on?" Harvey questioned. "Why are people singing but no sound is audible? Only about half the people here are even singing now."

Jesus nodded with frown. "I know. I'm showing you what it means to sing for my glory. It's not the voice I hear but the heart behind the words."

Diana sighed. "So the people that we can't hear aren't really worshipping?"

Jesus shook his head. "Nope. They're just wasting their time. They might as well not even have come. But they think that their presence here impresses me."

"And it doesn't, I take it?" spoke up Charles.

"No, it doesn't. In fact, not only doesn't it impress me, but it's sin. I hate it."

He gathered the group together, and they instantaneously found themselves in a contemporary worship service with a large band up front and people dancing in the aisles. It seemed to Diana that every hand in the place was in the air and almost every eye was closed.

Harvey covered his ears. "Can we go back to the 'Amazing Grace' people?"

Jesus laughed. "I just wanted to show Courtney that her guitar can be used for worship."

Courtney was smiling and even seemed to be getting into the song. Her hand was tapping her side as her head bobbed to the bass drum that was thumping their chests.

Jesus continued, "But like the other place, I don't hear all that you are."

Again the music was dampened as many of the voices and instruments suddenly cut out. Diana's eyes were fixed on a pair of teenage girls both jumping up and down beside each other with arms raised toward the ceiling. She couldn't help but notice that both of their actions were exactly the same, but only one of the girls' voices was able to be heard.

Jesus let his guests watch the service for a few minutes before regrouping them and bringing them back to the hotel.

"So you really hate the people that we couldn't hear?" asked Harvey, sitting down on one of the leather couches.

"I don't hate the people," Jesus explained, "just what they are doing."

"But at least they are in church," piped in Courtney. "Isn't that worth something?"

Jesus looked at her and shook his head.

"Imagine if a friend of yours came over to your house for a visit. You spent an hour having a nice conversation with them. Come to find out, everything they had said to you was a lie. How would you feel?"

All Courtney could do was nod.

"They could learn a lot from the birds," Charles declared, sneaking a wink toward Jesus.

Jesus chuckled. Harvey once again pried at Charles to tell him what all of this was about.

The host looked at Charles. "Why don't you tell them about our adventure? It would do them a lot of good."

"I don't think they would believe me."

"Try me," replied Harvey. "My mind is open to anything right now. We all just jumped into a picture of a church and were invisible to the attendees. What could be more unbelievable than that?"

"Well, let me tell ya," Charles answered with a smirk.

Diana didn't know what was happening to Charles, but he was subtly changing as they spent more time with Jesus. He was different from the snippy man at the bus stop. She liked the new Charles, but whatever was happening to the people around her left her with a very uneasy feeling.

She watched as the group gathered around him as he began. Courtney snuck closer to Jesus and whispered something to him.

"Charles, you can continue telling your story. Courtney and I will be back later."

Chapter 12

The two walked through the door into the dining room where the smell of supper still hovered in the air.

"I'm very confused," she started. "I guess I felt that I needed to talk to you more, and I really didn't want the others around when we did."

"I am very glad you want to talk more, Courtney. There is much to discuss. Let's start with your mom."

He sat down at the table as Courtney stopped in her tracks and glared.

"You just had to go there, didn't you?" she uttered.

"Listen, Cort, if we are to get anywhere with this conversation, we must start at the root of it all. And I am very aware that it is your mom. So, tell me about her."

"Well, where do I start? She is a control freak, hates everything I love, and only wants me around if I'm living out her dream for me."

"What does she hate that you love?"

Courtney sat down in the chair directly to Jesus's left.

"Music, Robbie, my dreams ..." she trailed off.

"What else?" he questioned.

"My clothes and every friend I've had."

Jesus nodded. "Have you ever thought that she may have disapproved of all these things because she cares for you? She doesn't want to run your life but only help guide it. She does love you, Courtney."

Courtney backed her chair farther away from the man sitting next to her.

"Are you on her side?" she exclaimed.

"No, child, I'm not on her side. I don't take sides. The only thing I am for is good relationships. I desire to see your mom and you become good friends again and to show love for each other."

"I really don't think that's going to happen. She ruined any chance of that. After she gave me the choice to either follow my dreams and leave her house or stay in school and be able to stay, she lost me. I will never go back to her."

Jesus's face remained somber as he watched her intently.

"How have you been dealing with having to state your fear just to enter your room?"

"I think it's cruel," she quickly replied.

"I did it for a reason. There is always something that controls our life. We may call it dreams or plans, but more times than not, it's fear. Every choice that you have made for the last few months has been rooted in the fear that you are wrong and your mother is right. So you are doing everything you can to prove her wrong. I brought you here to get away from everybody that is influencing your life and to come to grips with what is going on. You need guidance in your life. You need me."

"I know that you claim to be God and all that, but why you? Why should I trust my whole life to you?"

"I don't use fear to guide my people. I replace fear with freedom and doubts with security. My Spirit, which will be given to you if you just trust me, will be your comforter and helper. And as long as you rely on him, your life will be successful."

"Yeah, so you've said," she mumbled.

A silence formed between the two as she sat and thought hard about the words he had spoken to her. She knew he was right, and she hated him because of it. Every goal that she had was simply to show that she could run her own life.

She thought back to when her mother and she used to bake and talk together for hours. They were best friends and shared every little secret with each other. Quite often they sang together as she was learning the guitar.

Courtney's grim demeanor slowly changed to sadness as she suddenly missed the close relationship they used to have. It all had changed when she started up her first band with a few kids from school. And since her mom disapproved of it and demanded that she quit, her attitude toward her mother became hatred. So Courtney moved out.

"And then what happened to that band?" asked Jesus.

"Wha … wh … how did you know what I was thinking?"

He just smiled. "What happened?"

"After a few gigs, and a rising fan base, they found a better guitar player and replaced me."

Jesus scooted closer to the weeping girl and placed his hands over hers.

"My dear, your mother did not disapprove of your music. She was scared of who you were playing music with. She saw a change in your attitude, clothing, and focus. This band was only going to get you hurt, and she knew that. She was trying to protect you."

"And when I introduced her to Robbie …"

"Same thing. She knew he was trouble."

Courtney sat back and wiped her eyes. This man across from her had shown her what had been eating at her for some time now. The problem wasn't everybody else; it was herself.

"How do you know all of this?" she quietly asked.

"I am God," he stated. "I was with you through every stage of your life. I know because I was there. I saw it all. What I'm offering to you right now is for me to take control of your life. You have realized that you can't do it on your own. Your decisions have hurt you physically and emotionally. I want to lead you into joy, peace, and love. I want to show you what life is supposed to be lived like. I guarantee that it will not be boring like you always thought church people were like."

She snickered. "You heard me say that before too, I take it?"

"I sure did," he answered with a smirk. "Are you ready for a change, something different?"

She nodded, and this time she leaned over and grabbed his hands.

Looking him directly in the face, she whispered, "Show me what it's like to live without fear."

—

The old man dug in the bottom of his closet, throwing shoes out of the way. He crawled to the back, ducking under shirts and jackets that hung up above him, and grabbed an old briefcase. He hadn't used it in twenty-five years, but he now had a need for it again.

He emptied a shoe box of letters into the briefcase and grabbed one as they fell. Opening it, he read:

Dearest Harvey,

Love is an interesting thing. For years, all I ever worried about was me, but now, you are my every thought. Every dinner I cook, every piece of furniture I dust, and every article of clothing I fold, I do for you. It is the least I can do for a man that has treated me like a queen. I am writing this note and placing it in your lunchbox so you will get it at work. This is a simple thank you for the wonderful home you have provided for me and I hope that your egg salad and cheese sandwich will make you smile. I know it's your favorite! Be safe and come home to me soon.
With every heartbeat,
Annie

He began weeping. After placing it into the briefcase with the others, he reached for a small black Bible already on the bed. Annie had told him that he should read it with her, but he had always refused.

Opening to the page where the bookmark was kept, his eyes glanced over the words. A handwritten note in the margin specifically caught his eye.

Never stop praying!

He placed the Bible into the briefcase. Grabbing other mementos of Annie, including her wedding ring, favorite blouse, and journal, he closed it and headed out the door. If Annie couldn't be with him, this was as close as he could get. This briefcase would never again leave his side.

Jesus reentered the lobby to find three of the four remaining guests visiting as they looked at the pictures on the wall.

"Where is Madison?"

Startled, Diana turned her head to face the man standing across the room from her.

"She is in the recliner over there feeding Fern," she answered pointing in the direction of the black chairs.

A hand rose up and waved from behind one of the recliners.

"She's almost done," Madison yelled.

"Where's Courtney?" questioned Charles.

Jesus smiled.

Harvey took a deep breath. "Don't tell me that she's gone now too."

The host nodded and kept smiling.

The elderly man shook his head and scratched it.

"I know it's supposed to be a good thing, but I don't get it. I just don't get it. Something seems fishy about all this. No disrespect, sir, but I'm getting real nervous about all of this. One by one we all start disappearing. It seems like all of this is out of an Agatha Christie novel or something."

"Well," Jesus cut in, "while you are having your doubts, angels in heaven are rejoicing."

"But why should we believe you? You can do amazing things that I can't explain—send a man sliding up the railing and take us on trips through your artwork—but who is to say you don't have Louis and Courtney tied up in the basement or something? And what about Chester? I haven't seen him in a while."

"Annie is celebrating with them."

Harvey stopped short. Diana could see beads of sweat forming on his forehead starting to drip down from underneath his perfectly combed white hair. His eyes narrowed.

"What did you say?"

"I said—"

"I know what you said!" Harvey exclaimed. "How dare you bring my Annie into this! Don't you ever mention her again!"

Diana backed up against the nearest wall, wishing that she could just blend in and hide. Madison, looking equally as frightened, stood up and patted Fern on the back.

"You can say whatever you want about me, Jesus, but don't ever talk about my wife!"

Jesus walked a little closer to the group while never looking away from Harvey.

Shaking his head, he answered, "Why can't I mention her, Harvey? I love her more than you do."

"H … h … how?" he asked, stuttering over his words now. "How can you love her more than I do? For fifty-three years we were happily married. My life's purpose was solely to make sure she was happy. She was my life! And now …"

Jesus walked even closer until he was an arm's reach from the man who looked as if he wanted to punch him.

"I created her," he explained. "And I loved her so much that I died in her place. I couldn't stand the thought of being separated from her forever. And now I don't have to be. She hasn't been with me too long yet but we have sure enjoyed each other so far."

The elderly man glared at Jesus. "She is with you? She is dead! Don't you get it? If you are God, then you took her from me! She was everything to me. Quit talking about her!"

Suddenly his face went blank. Diana watched helplessly as he grabbed at his chest and gasped for air. Then as suddenly as he stopped yelling, his body crashed to the floor.

Chapter 13

"Harvey?"

Madison's words were the only thing that could be heard in the room. All stood in shock as they watched Jesus kneel beside the fallen man. Relief flooded over Diana as she spotted Harvey's chest move slowly up and down.

"He's alive," stated Jesus, looking toward Charles. "I need your help to get him into a bed. He needs medical attention."

Charles joined him on the floor.

"How are we going to get him up the stairs?"

"We aren't. Just help me carry him to the room off of the dining room."

The two men grunted and moaned as they carried the dead weight of the elderly man across the lobby, into the dining room, and through the door.

Inside was a hospital room with the bed, chairs, and all the equipment you would see in any hospital.

"So that's what is in this room," said Charles, barely getting his words out as he helped lay Harvey in the bed.

Jesus looked around at it.

"Oh, this room is anything I need it to be."

A lady with short, black, curly hair walked in and starting checking all of his vitals. Harvey didn't move during the whole process but only wheezed with each breath.

"Everyone, this is Myra. She is going to be his nurse."

Only faint "hi's" and "hey's" came from the group, who were still speechless from the sudden turn of events. It seemed so long ago now, but Diana remembered the bus ride here and her first encounter with Harvey and his outgoing personality. It was the first, and one of the very few times, that she felt comfortable since she left her house.

Her house! She hadn't even thought about poor Duke. This trip had been taking a lot longer than she had planned. She hoped that he was all right. His dish was overflowing with food when she left and the neighbors were to keep an eye out for him, but worries nevertheless overcame her.

"Myra will take good care of him, I promise. We should all get some rest. Harvey needs some anyway."

His words cut through her wandering thoughts. Charles grabbed Jesus's arm as he walked by him toward the door. Diana caught a glimpse of the old Charles again as he stood firm looking deep into the host's eyes.

"What you said did this to him. Why did you get him so worked up?"

Jesus peered over his shoulder and took one final caring look toward the man in the bed now hooked up to IVs and monitors.

The host removed Charles's hand from his arm, gave him one last look, and said as he left, "You'll see."

—

Sand was all Diana could see in every direction. She stood and brushed off her jeans and t-shirt. She squinted in the direction of the sun as it blazed down upon her. Her helpless situation left a tight knot in her stomach. She didn't know where she was, how she got there, or where she was supposed to go. The wind took her breath away and blew sand into her eyes.

She rubbed them with her hands until she could see again. When her sight refocused, she noticed two footprints in front of her, twice as large as her feet were. She frowned as she knelt down and traced one with her finger.

Standing again, she placed her feet into the two mysterious prints. Immediately, two more appeared in front of her. She quickly moved into those as well and again more appeared.

With sand whipping her across the face, she followed the tracks across the desert. As long as she continued moving, she forgot about the wind and the sand and concentrated on her journey.

But then they stopped. She stood in the large footprints but before her was only blowing sand. She looked around, helpless, still just as lost as before. Tears formed as she screamed for help even though she knew nobody could hear her. But just when she felt completely powerless, two tracks formed in the sand right beside her. They weren't as large as the previous pair, but still much larger than her own.

They doubled as two more appeared directly in front of the others. She followed alongside, and they continued to be produced in the sand. When they turned, she turned along with them. When they traveled straight, she walked straight.

She glanced up to see if she could see anything. Off in the distance there seemed to be two very short people waiting for her. She looked down but the tracks had stopped. Ignoring the stinging sand beating across her body, she ran toward the two unknown people.

Getting closer, she realized they weren't short, but were kneeling. She finally was able to focus on their faces as she got closer, and the shock left her breathless. On their knees before her were Jim and her father, both gagged and handcuffed. They looked at her wearily, obviously having been trying to escape for some time now.

Diana noticed a small three-legged table in front of the two men. On top of it sat two objects: a revolver and a key. The two men's attentions were torn between the table and the woman standing before them. She picked up the key and walked behind the men. It definitely would fit in the locks of the handcuffs, but she walked back in front of them.

Removing their gags, she stepped back and tapped the key on the table. Rage filled her as she stared at the two men of her life.

"Diana, unlock us. Please!"

She looked into the face of her pathetic father as he commanded her to free him.

"Listen to him, dear. Let us go!"

Her face remained unchanged as her hand set down the key and picked up the gun. She rubbed the barrel with the other hand as she looked back at her husband.

"Why should I let either one of you go?" she asked, checking the gun closely.

There were two rounds in the chamber. She closed it back up and cocked it.

She looked back at the two men now sweating in fear.

"Diana, I'm your father! This is crazy! Just unlock the cuffs!"

"My father," she retorted with a laugh. "You are my father, huh? You passed on your genes to me. That makes you my father, but you were not my dad.

"I am not going into this with you right now. We've talked about it and I apologized. What else do you want!"

"I want you to be a dad! That's what I want!"

"You are acting nuts," interrupted Jim. "Put that gun down and unlock us. Come on. We can talk later."

"Oh," she laughed, "Talking. Oh yes, you are good at talking, aren't you? You are all talk! Why don't you go to your girlfriend's house and talk with her? I'm sure she's a great conversationalist!"

"That's enough!" he bit back. "That was a mistake. I've already said I'm sorry."

"A mistake? A *mistake!* You were having an affair for three months! That is not a mistake, Jim! That's a choice!"

She pointed the revolver only three inches from his forehead. She was never as angry as she was at this moment. Her finger twitched as tears poured from her eyes.

"Diana, put that gun down right now!" yelled her father. "Quit acting like a fool! Just let us go and we can work this entire thing out!"

She pointed the gun at him and sobbed through her words.

"Work this entire thing out? You are already gone! It's too late for us! I'm sick of all of this. You two have ruined my life! I'm done!"

Two gunshots rang out through the desert storm.

—

Her body jolted as she gasped for air. Sweat soaked her shirt as she tried to catch her breath.

Beep. Beep. Beep.

"Are you okay?" whispered a voice to her left.

She straightened herself up in the chair that she had slept in all night. Diana had refused to leave Harvey's side when all of the others had retired to their rooms. The weak man tried to sit up slightly as he stared at the frightened woman.

"Did you have a nightmare?" he asked.

She nodded as she ran her hands through her hair.

"I seem to have them a lot here," she sighed.

He groaned and lay back down. "This place is turning into a nightmare. What time is it?"

Diana just looked at him.

"Yeah, right. There is no time."

They sat silently for a while. The two gunshots still echoed in Diana's mind as the dream played over and over through her head. How could she have shot them? She would never do such a thing.

Clearing her head, she walked to Harvey's bedside.

"How are you feeling?"

Harvey took a shallow breath. "I feel like somebody shot me in the chest. Sharp pains dart through my body every time I move."

Diana shuddered at his analogy. She quickly pushed the images of her father and husband out of her head.

"So, Harvey, was Annie your wife?"

"Yes."

"How long were you two married?"

"Fifty-three years." He smiled. "Fifty-three wonderful years."

She repeated the number under her breath. Grabbing her chair, she sat down next to his adjustable bed.

"Harvey, I've been married for only seventeen years. Fifty-three isn't even in my reality. How did you last that long with one person?"

He laughed but sat up slightly as a coughing fit overtook him.

When he caught his breath, he smiled and answered, "The problem is that I wouldn't refer to it as lasting, my dear. Life isn't life if you are merely surviving. It's the same with marriage. Marriage is truly marriage when you enjoy every moment."

"But we have grown into two completely different people," she complained.

"Well, Diana, I am so glad Annie was completely different from me. I would never stay with somebody like me. I would drive myself insane!"

She laughed and nodded. "Okay, you got me there."

"Listen," he said, leaning more so he could face her better. "I'm not saying that every day in our marriage was paradise. We had our days of anger and disagreements, but my wife was a saint. She always reminded me to think of each other more than ourselves."

"That sounds like good advice."

"Oh, I'm sure it was," he grinned. "It was that darn church she attended. They told her that was one way of keeping a relationship in check. I suppose it worked."

"So she was a Christian?" she asked.

"Yeah, she was. It made her happy. I didn't mind if she attended. It definitely wasn't my thing. If you ask me, the man who owns this place is a quack. He's up to something …"

The door opened at that moment. Jesus walked in, looking at Harvey with Myra close on his heels.

"Good morning," he said as he entered, smiling at the two startled guests.

"Good morning," they repeated simultaneously. Diana wasn't sure if it really was though.

Myra immediately began checking Harvey's vitals. She looked concerned but said nothing.

"Diana, you should go upstairs and get ready for breakfast. The others will be down any minute," Jesus said quietly.

—

The shower felt good after sleeping in a chair all night. The only thing that the water couldn't wash away was the thoughts that were haunting her; the nightmares, the missing people, and the man who called himself Jesus. She allowed the hot water to pour over her longer than usual. In the quietness of the moment, she tried to pray but the words just wouldn't come. Her fears suddenly overwhelmed her. She dropped to her knees and began to cry. Her body convulsed as she wept harder than she had in a long time. She gasped for air between sobs, and tears rushed down her cheeks as fast as the shower water was.

After regaining control, she got dressed and then looked in the mirror at her eyes, only slightly swollen now. She took a few deep breaths, combed out her hair, and turned to leave.

Walking downstairs, she saw the others already partaking in the alluring breakfast consisting of pancakes, eggs, various meats, and potatoes. Nobody said much until they were all finished eating.

"How's Harvey?" Charles asked. "Jesus told us that you stayed with him all night."

"So it's for sure Jesus, huh?" Diana asked, slightly joking.

"Well, it's easier to say than mysterious, all-knowing, magic-working stranger," he answered with a wink.

They all laughed. They all needed to laugh. It felt good.

"To answer your question, I have no idea how he is doing. He was talking to me before the nurse came in, but he had a bad cough and I could tell it hurt for him to move. The nurse seemed a little concerned with some of his vitals as well. But I don't know any more than that."

Burping Fern over her left shoulder, Madison chimed in, "Harvey sure got upset last night."

"Yeah, Annie was his wife."

"Yeah, I figured that," commented Charles.

Just then Jesus walked out of the adjoining room.

"I trust all of you slept well, even if it was in a chair," he said, grinning at Diana. "Diana and Charles, I have something for you to read. Please go up to your rooms and spend an hour or so looking it over."

"What is it?" questioned Charles.

"It's a letter a friend of mine wrote many, many years ago. I think it would be beneficial for each of you to read it. Don't mind if you don't understand it all. I will answer your questions later."

"What about me?" asked Madison.

He smiled, "Madison, you need to come with me. We have lots to discuss."

Chapter 14

Myra came walking into the dining room and passed by Diana and Charles as they left for their bedrooms.

"Madison, may Myra watch Fern until we get back?" Jesus asked. "Our discussion will go much smoother if you don't have to carry her everywhere."

Myra reached for Fern, but Madison grabbed her tighter and took a couple of steps backward, bumping into the dining room table.

"I promise not to hurt her, dear," the nurse calmly spoke. "I won't take my eyes off of her. She will be completely safe with me."

"You can trust her," Jesus said.

"I don't know," whispered Madison nervously. "I want to trust you both. I really do. I don't know …"

Myra stepped toward the hesitant mother once again. This time Madison allowed her baby into the arms of the soft-spoken woman.

She smiled. "I will be right here with her when you return. I promise."

Jesus took Madison's hand and led her toward the door behind which Harvey lay.

"Come now," Jesus commanded. "The sooner we leave the sooner we will return."

Fern found the lady's buttons very interesting and was trying to get them into her mouth.

Madison asked, "Why are we going back into that room? Shouldn't Harvey rest?"

Turning the knob, Jesus smiled. "Oh, Harvey won't be where we're going."

—

The two walked through the door and directly into a very busy grocery store. Madison was among fast-moving carts and people all bustling up and down the aisles. She could faintly hear classical music playing overhead above the loud roar of the shoppers.

Madison looked back, and the door was no longer there. Jesus saw the confused look on her face and placed his hand on her shoulder.

"I told you. This room is whatever I need it to be."

"We need to go grocery shopping?" inquired the young woman.

"No we don't," Jesus said, laughing. "We are here to discuss you and your past. You have spoken unfair criticisms against me. I want to get things cleared up."

They both saw a woman pushing a cart down the aisle toward them. In the cart was a young girl bouncing up and down. She was screaming at the top of her lungs, and her red-faced mother was trying to push the cart, look for groceries, and calm her daughter down all at the same time.

"I want a candy bar!" screamed the boisterous child. *"I want it now!"*

"Honey," spoke the mother under her breath while grabbing the back of the girl's shirt to sit her back down, "I said no candy today. We are going to have dinner soon, and you don't need to be eating sweets right now. Sit down!"

"I want candy! I want candy!" continued the unruly girl.

Then everything paused. The only two moving were Jesus and Madison. The little girl, frozen with her arms up in the air and her mouth wide open, was finally silent.

"What would you do in a time like this?" questioned Jesus.

"What do you mean?" asked Madison in return.

"I mean, if you were that mother, what would you do?"

"I don't know, discipline her somehow I guess."

"Okay, but how specifically? Just answer honestly. I promise this isn't a test on how good of a mother you are or what are proper ways of discipline. You will see why I'm asking soon."

She sighed. "I would leave the shopping cart right where it is, take the girl out to the car, and drive home. When we got home, I would spank her and remind her that she will never talk like that to me again, especially in a public place. She probably wouldn't get candy for a few days either."

Jesus looked at her. "Okay. Now come with me."

They walked past all the people still frozen in various positions. Madison bumped into a man bent over reaching for a bag of potato chips.

"Oops!" she uttered.

She reached for him in case he fell over but the statue-like man remained stationary. Dodging in and out of the unmoving shoppers, they headed straight for the front doors and walked through as they opened automatically. As soon as they passed through, they found themselves in a living room.

On a loveseat sat a long-haired teenage boy clearly upset. His head was down and his arms were crossed over his chest. A man, who Diana guessed was the father, sat in a recliner across the room from him. A heated discussion was taking place as Jesus and Madison walked in.

Madison felt very uncomfortable. She felt like she was intruding on something that she shouldn't have been witnessing.

"Dad, I hate your stupid rules! I want to go with Bobby tonight!"

"I told you that you aren't going. There is no discussion here. You didn't respect your mother today, and I told you that if you ever yelled at her again that you would have privileges taken away. I'm sorry, Pete, but rules are rules, no matter how stupid they may seem."

The boy just stared at the floor. Finally standing, he pointed a finger at his father.

"I hate you. You can keep me here tonight, but you can't keep me here forever. One day you will wake up and I won't be here. Then you will regret ever making those stupid rules."

The man glared. "Don't threaten me. Get to your room now. I don't want to see your face until morning."

The teenager stomped down the hall, and Madison heard a door slam. The man sat back in his chair, and a tear made a path down his cheek.

Jesus turned to her. "So how did he do?"

Madison choked up thinking about Fern. She knew she was making up this mother thing. Parenthood didn't come natural to her, and she feared this very scene in the future. She hoped it would never happen.

"He stuck to his guns, I suppose. That's all he could do. I know that you have to act on your promises, and if he threatened with no privileges, then he had to follow through with it."

"I agree," Jesus quietly said. "It's not always easy, though, is it?"

"No." It was all she could say.

Jesus grabbed her hand and directed her toward the front door. Walking through, she gasped.

She found herself in a church foyer looking directly at a group of four women she recognized very well, one of which was her. There was Tammy, Yvonne, and Nadia with their "holier than thou" faces on, pointing fingers directly at Madison.

"We can't have people like you ruining the image of our friendly church. We ask that you leave!"

She watched herself weep and beg to stay. She began to tear up, remembering the horrible encounter she had with that church.

"I don't want to watch this, Jesus."

"But it's very important we clear this up," he reminded her.

"I knew I made a mistake, and I admitted it to these ladies, who I thought were my friends. I never intended to sleep with Professor Reynolds," she confessed, now crying harder. "And obviously the pregnancy was an accident too. But what I thought I would receive from the ladies was the exact opposite. They told me to leave the church!"

Jesus just nodded. "I know. It doesn't give me pleasure to make you relive this moment, but I knew that we needed to if we were to have a relationship. I won't make you stay much longer."

He stretched his arm around her shoulders and gave her a gentle hug as she wiped tears from her face with the back of her hand.

"I suppose you're right," she continued. "I hated anything that had to do with God from then on. Not only were these people hypocrites, but the God they served must be one too. I wasn't even sure if he existed at all."

"Why do you think I showed you the first two places before bringing you here?"

She shrugged. Madison had been wondering that as well. She watched herself walk out the door of the church as the ladies shook their heads and mumbled among themselves.

"I showed you two instances where the parents needed to or were disciplining their children. You admitted it needed to be done and even commended the father for doing so even though it broke his heart."

He paused, looking up at the three women still talking quietly to each other.

"I love those three women. They are my children, but what they did to you was inexcusable. They are supposed to represent me with their lives, but they didn't. When children disobey, the parents are obligated to discipline them so they will once again obey. Let me assure you, these three ladies did not get away scot free with their actions."

"What did you do to them?" Madison asked.

"Honestly, the mode of discipline isn't important. The fact is that they suffered for hurting you. But you never knew that. It wasn't me that kicked you out; it was rebellious children of mine. And on behalf of them, I'm sorry."

"It broke your heart to punish them, didn't it?"

"Yes it did. But it didn't break my heart as bad as to see you run away from me."

"Do you blame me?" she inquired. "The only thing I knew about God was these people and they failed me."

He continued, "I brought other people into your life since then in attempts to draw you back to myself."

The room suddenly changed to a bus station where Madison again saw herself, but this time much more pregnant. She was sitting on a bench waiting and looking very uncomfortable.

"I remember this," she said to Jesus. "A man will come along and offer a pillow for me to sit on. But then he gets all preachy with me."

"Yes, that is right. His name is Lance. His kind action led to a conversation with you about me. But your heart was still hard and you wouldn't listen."

The room changed again and this time they found Madison laying in a hospital bed only a couple of hours before Fern would enter the world. A nurse walked in and offered Madison a hand to hold.

"May I pray for you, dear?" the nurse asked softly.

"Sure," answered Madison.

Jesus pointed at the nurse. "Her name is Barbara. I made sure that she was your nurse so that you would have a godly woman looking after you. She was very kind, wasn't she?"

Madison nodded.

"Her kindness softened your heart a little. I won't take you to every instance I spoke into your heart through my servants, but be assured that there were many more. It wasn't until I believed that you were ready that I called you to meet me here. I hope you see that those church women were not acting like Christians. They didn't represent me at all. I didn't want you to leave that church and walk away from me. I didn't do that to you."

"Just like the father who sent his boy to his room for disrespecting his mom ..." she started.

He continued, "That was like me punishing those women for not loving you as they should. They were selfish like the little girl in the grocery store, only wanting what they wanted. But I didn't give up on you, and I still am the loving God that you heard about. I promise."

She didn't say anything else. He led her to the hospital room door, and they walked through into the familiar dining room. Myra and Fern were laughing as she was playing peek-a-boo with her hands.

Giving Myra a slight smile, Madison stooped down and scooped Fern up into her arms. The baby wrapped her arms around Madison's body, giving her a hug.

"Thank you," she said to the nurse.

"My pleasure dear," she replied.

Her face suddenly went stern as an alarm started ringing throughout the house. Madison jumped and quickly moved aside as Myra ran into the adjoining room, the door slamming behind her.

Chapter 15

But thanks be to God that though you were slaves of sin, you became obedient from the heart to that form of teaching to which you were committed. And having been freed from sin, you became slaves of righteousness. I am speaking in human terms because of the weakness of your flesh. For just as you presented your members as slaves to impurity and to lawlessness, resulting in further lawlessness, so now present your members as slaves to righteousness, resulting in sanctification.

Diana set down the letter onto the bed in front of her. Leaning her back against the wall, she sighed.

"Don't mind if you don't understand it all. I will answer your questions later."

His words echoed in her confused mind. So many questions were still left unanswered. She had to have been reading for at least an hour by her calculations, but it seemed to have flown by. This letter, although extremely complex, grasped her attention and wouldn't let go. The words were not just affecting her mind, but her whole being was being moved by the words.

She thought back to fond memories of her mother reading her the Bible before bed. There were some interesting stories, but for the most part the Bible bored her. She didn't care what her mother was reading; it was her soothing voice that lulled her to sleep.

She rolled over and picked up the frame holding the picture of her parents and her. Removing the photo of her younger father and the baby, she again looked at the picture that had caused her so much grief earlier. She looked into the beautiful green eyes of her mother. Sadness swept over her as a longing for her mother came over her. She had been so focused on her father the past few days that she had forgotten about the amazing woman who had raised her.

"Mom, I hope I'm making you proud," she whispered to the photo.

An alarm caused her whole body to freeze. After the sudden shock wore off, she bolted for the door, running into a very pale Charles.

"What is that horrible noise?" she asked him.

Just shrugging, he passed by her and tore down the stairs. They both reached the bottom just in time to see Jesus and Madison heading through the door into Harvey's room.

Quickly following them, they found Myra, Jesus, and Madison standing around the bed looking at the old man. The alarm had finally shut off and the two quietly entered and followed suit.

"I've got him stable but I'm not sure if he has much longer. His body seems to be giving up on us," Myra said mainly to the host of the hotel.

"Harvey, don't give up on us yet," Jesus said to the sick man in a commanding voice. "We aren't finished."

"Finished?" questioned Charles. "He can't die, can he? I mean, we are in your presence. He can't die here!"

Without acknowledging Charles, Jesus continued. "Harvey, I mentioned Annie because I knew that you needed to know that she is okay. She hopes that you will join her soon. I heard prayers from her every day of her married life with you. That is why I called you here."

Harvey opened his eyes partway and slowly turned his head Jesus's way. He groaned and closed his eyes again.

"Harvey, I have introduced myself to you many times in your years of life but you have ignored me every time. Your heart has been extremely hard toward me, but I can sense that I have broken through."

His eyes opened again. "How can you sense that?" his scratchy voice asked.

"Well, you are finally talking to me," he answered with a grin. "I think it's time for a much-needed conversation."

"I'm really in no mood to talk."

Diana's heart broke as she watched a man she barely knew become weaker and weaker. His voice was faint, and his actions were extremely slow and looked very painful.

Jesus looked into his bloodshot eyes as if he was reading his thoughts.

"Harvey, what if your last breath isn't too far away? Don't you think you should talk with me? I know you have issues with me that you need to get off of your chest. Why didn't you serve me like Annie did? What about me did you not like?"

The old man looked back at him and sighed.

"Fine. I'll talk to you," he whispered. "There are things that I can't stand about you. My wife loved you, and I was okay with that. It gave her a community of friends and a hope. But I like to think of myself as an intellectual and didn't buy into this faith thing. I'm not putting my faith in anyone who lies."

His words came slow and painfully. Each syllable came with a shortness of breath.

"Lies?" questioned Jesus raising his eyebrows. "When did I ever lie?"

The man let out a snort and raised himself up a bit more.

"Let's start with your book. Annie would tell me that it was God's very words speaking to us. But I heard enough of it throughout my life to know that it contradicts itself. And if Jesus is the so-called truth, then Jesus is a liar."

"Do you have any examples of these contradictions, Harvey?"

Diana slid backward until she was leaning against the wall. The tension in the air was stiff, and fear swept over her. She met eyes with Madison, who seemed equally as tense. She crept silently beside Diana and grabbed her hand.

"Well, yes, in fact, I do have an example," the old man wheezed. "The same book tells us to take an eye for an eye and a tooth for a tooth. But then later God tells his people to turn the other cheek and love their enemies. Now, Jesus, which one are we supposed to do?"

The man ended his question with a deep, hoarse cough.

Jesus answered him, "You are correct in saying that both of those commands are in the Scriptures. But you have lost the context of each one and whom they were spoken to. I gave a man named Moses the Law to give to the Hebrew nation. I chose them out of my sovereignty to be the nation into which I would be born. This Law was very strict in its expectations for the people and its punishment if they disobeyed. Under the Law, it did say to take an eye for an eye and a tooth for a tooth. I didn't do this just to be harsh but to show them how terrible sin really is. The consequences are so severe that they can't truly be understood unless they had to live it out. If any of the people could have followed all of the laws their whole life without messing up, they could have entered heaven. But only I succeeded in doing so. The rest of them failed and so suffered the punishment of disobeying me. It sounds cruel, but you must understand the bad news to truly appreciate the good. The full purpose of the Law was to lead them to me. Only by grace can any of them enter my presence in heaven. The Law proved that they weren't good enough and needed help in order to be saved. Understand that now?"

The old man nodded. "That makes sense, but who did you command to love their enemies?"

Jesus continued, never looking away from Harvey.

"That command was for the church. Israel was my chosen people to whom I revealed myself and used to reach others. But they rejected me and so I then chose to reveal myself to the entire world and use any of them to do my work. If anybody will put their faith in me, the Comforter will indwell them, and they will immediately become a part of my church. But the church isn't under the Law. My death and resurrection fulfilled the Law. It no longer has control. Now the people live under grace, not under a set of rules."

"What is grace?" piped up Madison.

Jesus looked up at her. "Do you remember when your English professor gave you a second chance on your final exam after you failed the first one?"

Madison nodded.

"You didn't deserve a second chance, but she gave you one. You asked and she agreed. That was grace—receiving something wonderful that you could never earn and surely don't deserve."

Charles then spoke up. "So having our sins forgiven is undeserved. That is why it's called grace?"

Jesus smiled. "You are all finally understanding."

Turning back to Harvey, he continued his explanation.

"So since the Law was now no longer enacted and all of the church is now living in grace, their actions should show grace, not the Law. I want my people to live out what they believe. Since they have been forgiven of all things, they should forgive everybody else of all things. It only makes sense. They have been recreated at the moment of their conversion, and their new self has the ability to love and forgive others the same way I did for them."

"Recreated, huh? Is that why Annie called herself a born-again Christian?" Harvey asked.

"That's exactly why," Jesus replied. "Do you see now that the Bible doesn't contradict itself? Anything you may bring up can be explained."

The man lay back down completely and stared at the ceiling. His hands were folded on his chest, and each breath took much energy.

"Well, you may have answered that, but I still have doubts. I survived a war that was anything but wonderful. I saw three of my best friends shot down in front of me. I carried them to safety only to have them die right before my eyes. Jack asked me to personally say good-bye to his wife for him. So many people died ..." his voice trailed off.

Nobody spoke but just kept their eyes on the old man. He eventually spoke up again.

"I hear on the news all the time of catastrophe after catastrophe. Thousands of people are dying in earthquakes, children all over the world are dying of AIDS, and it seems like every family on the planet is affected by cancer. You tell me, Jesus, how can a God that is all-loving and all-powerful allow such tragedies? It seems so cruel. Explain that."

Jesus's face turned very somber. He reached over and laid his right hand upon Harvey's folded hands.

"I grieved your losses with you, Harvey. You have to realize that death wasn't my idea. When I created the world, it was perfect. People were without sin, had a perfect relationship with me, and would never even know what death was. But they decided that they knew better than I did and chose to disobey. The moment they did, death entered the world. Harvey, death means separation. They were separated from me from that moment on and for the first time, started to die physically as well. Each life to be born from then on would experience physical death as well, separation of the spirit from the body. So the fact that death is happening all around is not my fault. It breaks my heart, it really does. Do I have the power to stop things from happening? Of course I do."

"Then why don't you?" Harvey questioned, butting in.

"If I stopped every bad thing from happening in this world, everybody would have a great life—one without worries, doubts, pain, or trauma."

"That would be great," Charles commented under his breath.

Jesus looked his direction.

"It seems like that would be true. But if people never worried about a thing, never struggled in relationships or finances, or never experienced illnesses or pain, they would be extremely content with the way they were. The problem is that no matter how great their life is, there is still a huge problem. They are still separated from me. So although they live the easy life now, when they pass away from this earth, they will find themselves in a horrible place of torment forever and ever. Harvey, I allow things to happen in this world to show people that they need to be dependent on me. Grievous times drop people to their knees and many times straight to me. When a lady finds out she has breast cancer, it's amazing how fast she will start praying. When a great tragedy hits a city or a nation, the churches start filling up. I need you to understand that even though these horrific events seem uncharacteristic of me, I'm still there and waiting for people to run into my arms. Because if they never turn to me, I don't care how perfect their life seems to be, doom awaits them."

Harvey remained silent.

"What you never heard was the end of the story of your friend Jack Long. He died in your arms on the battlefield, and his wife back home wanted to die as well when she received the news. But a neighbor took her under her wing and using her tragedy, introduced her to Christ. She was told that God had died for her and that his Father experienced great heartache watching his only Son pass away on the cross. Because of the terrible death of your friend, his wife was saved. And through her, his sons and mother were also reached. Good came from that horrible event."

"And so there is a reason that you took Annie too then?" he whispered through his sobs.

"So you would see the void in your life. She was everything to you, but when she was removed, you realized how empty you were. I love you,

Harvey. I really do. Annie is alive in heaven with me and hopes to be with you again."

He paused and then continued. "What was your greatest fear?"

The man turned to face him and just stared.

"Why?" he finally murmured.

The host smiled and pointed to everybody else. "Look around you."

The old man's eyes bounced from person to person. He began weeping aloud, huge gasps wheezing from his lungs as he cried.

Diana started crying too even though she wasn't quite sure why.

"What was his fear?" questioned Charles.

Jesus answered him without taking his gaze off of the dying man.

"He didn't want to die alone."

The old man's hands grasped Jesus's hand so tightly that his knuckles turned white. Through his gasping, he barely got out the words.

"I'm sorry for being hard. My whole life was a waste! I need you. I believe you, Jesus. I really do."

The machine he was hooked to suddenly sounded an alarm, showing that he had flat lined. Myra quickly went to his side and checked his breathing and looked for a pulse.

Shaking her head, she uttered the words Diana was hoping that they would avoid.

"He's gone."

Chapter 16

Sitting at the dining room table, Diana said nothing, absolutely stunned by the previous events. She had watched Myra cover Harvey with a sheet and wheel the bed out of the room. Where they went, she wasn't sure. But she only made it to the dining room before needing to sit down.

Charles too sat at the table equally as silent. Madison took Fern upstairs, who was crying just as hard as her mother. She didn't know where Jesus had gone, but if she was honest, she was glad he wasn't around. There were many questions she wanted to ask of him, but now wasn't the time. She couldn't even talk without beginning to weep again.

Jesus had just finished talking about the horrible things that happen in life and explained why he allows them to happen. It had made sense at the time. But then, she was thrown for a loop when Harvey took his last breath.

After much time, the sound of footsteps coming down the stairs jerked both of their heads up to see who it was. They watched Madison, hair a complete mess and tear stains down her face, slowly creep down the spiral staircase hugging Fern tightly.

She sat down between the two other guests but remained silent. They all stayed motionless staring at each other in shock. It even seemed Fern was exceptionally still as well.

Another set of footsteps sounded from the staircase as Jesus came walking down toward the somber group. All three watched him quietly as he joined them at the table.

"I know this came as a surprise ..." he started, breaking the silence.

"Surprise is an understatement," Charles quickly shot back. "You let him die. I've heard the Bible stories, Jesus. You are supposedly a miracle worker. What happened?"

Diana jumped in. "Yeah, it seems like anytime somebody was very sick, close to death, or was actually dead around you that you healed them. Why didn't you do that for Harvey?"

Madison remained motionless. "I liked him."

Jesus nodded. "I did perform many miracles but they all had a purpose beyond just the immediate circumstances of the people ..."

"Why did you let Harvey die?"

Charles's outburst shook each member around the table. His direct question was exactly what Diana had wanted to ask.

Jesus leaned forward with a very serious expression.

"I hate death. Never in my plan for mankind did it include death. Man brought that upon himself. I told Adam the consequences for disobeying me, but curiosity was too much for him and his wife. I never wanted anybody to experience death. In fact, I didn't want anybody to even know what death meant!"

The passion and intensity of his words captivated the three remaining guests.

"But that is the past and death is reality now. And it wasn't physical death that I was even concerned about. It was the spiritual death; the spiritual separation from me. My relationship with Adam was severed. People often think of the Old Testament God as mean and vicious. But let me assure you, when I kicked the two out of Paradise, I mourned; I mourned deeply for what had transpired."

"That's why you had to die, right?" Madison questioned. "Because disobedience brought death and because you died, we don't have to now."

Jesus smiled. "I couldn't have said it better myself."

His smile quickly faded. "The death I undertook was almost too much to bear. Even being completely God in the flesh, that separation from the Father hurt more than the thorns piercing my skull and the nails burrowing through the nerves of my body. But in my own power, I conquered death. It's up to every person now to decide whether or not they want to live in victory or still be stung by the viciousness of death."

"I've heard the quote that those who are in Christ will never taste death," stated Diana, remembering back to her childhood church attendance. "I thought for sure Harvey trusted in you as he lay in that bed. But then he died. How do you explain that?"

"He did believe in me," the host responded. "And although his flesh passed away, Harvey never saw death. His spirit joined me in heaven, where he is more than alive and well. You see, in your perspective, the best thing for Harvey was keeping him here. I knew that the best thing for him was just letting him go. He would tell you the same thing right now."

"What about us?" Charles asked.

"What about you?"

"So Louis and Courtney and Harvey are all gone and supposedly better off but we are still here. What about us?"

Jesus stood and turned to leave.

Looking over his shoulder he spoke as he left, "That, Charles, is completely up to you.

—

Her first day of college was frightening, with hundreds of other students whom she didn't know, and already homework on the first day. She sat down in her final class of the day wishing it was already over.

Her father had promised to pay her way if she had decided to attend. She was excited to begin a new stage of her life but was nervous to leave the comfortable life that she had at home. She took a deep breath as the professor began to speak from the front of the classroom.

"Good afternoon. I'm Professor Reynolds. If you are not supposed to be in World Religions, I'd suggest panicking and heading for the door right now."

Laughter filled the air. The humor eased Madison's mind, and she smiled. Maybe this would be a good year after all.

—

Diana tossed and turned in her bed, causing small waves to pass beneath her body. Complete exhaustion was forcing her to fall asleep, but fear of what stayed hidden in her mind and appeared in her dreams won the battle and caused her to just lay there helpless. Getting out of bed, she headed for her door. She didn't know quite where she was going, but anything was better than laying there letting her thoughts control her.

She was still sad because of Harvey's death. She missed her children incredibly, and the thought of how to leave this place scared her most of all. Entering the lobby, she was able to make her way to a couch because of the slight blue moonlight that shone through the massive windows. A fire was still burning, and she lost herself staring into the bouncing flames.

"Can't sleep?"

Diana twisted her head to see a silhouette of a man standing in front of the giant windows.

"No."

Jesus came and sat beside her on the couch. He allowed a few silent moments to pass before continuing.

"It's your dreams, right?"

Without leaving her gaze on the flames, she nodded.

"How do you know about those?" she asked.

She asked the question but she didn't really care about the answer. Not much astonished her anymore. She was becoming numb to the constant surprises.

"I placed those dreams in your head."

She turned to face him, startled by what he said.

"You placed them in my head?" she repeated. "Why would you do a thing like that? These dreams have haunted me since I've been here. They have caused me to not even want to fall asleep."

It was his turn to nod. "I know. But it was an opportunity to teach you something. While you are asleep, I have your full attention."

Anger was beginning to rise in her petite body.

"What could you have possibly been teaching me through those horrible nightmares?"

"Well the first two were very similar. You struggle with men because of the father you had. He wasn't one. You never felt loved growing up. So when he neglected you, I wanted to show you that I was there. I was the Father looking out for you even when your father was not. I held you and protected you many times from people and things that could have hurt you."

"Why did you give me that photo of my father?" she interrupted.

He smiled. "How did it make you feel?"

"Good. I never knew anything that had to do with him could make me feel good."

"You needed that photo to reassure you that you were loved. It has softened your anger toward your father. But when you look at that photo from now on, I want you to see yourself being held by the compassionate arms of God."

She remained silent for a bit. The explanation of her last dream was coming, but she didn't want to hear it. She knew it couldn't be good.

"You had one more dream, didn't you?"

Her jaw tightened and then loosened as she popped her little finger into her mouth and began biting on the nail.

"I don't want to know what that one meant ..." she quietly said, trailing off.

"But the meaning is important," he continued. "You must learn this lesson."

She quickly left the couch and leaned against one of the majestic windows. She could only see the reflection of the flames in the glass, but she stared nonetheless. The meaning was something she could do without. The reason she shot the two most important men her life could not be good. She knew that for sure.

"Have you ever read the Bible?" he asked.

She turned, surprised by the question. It took her a moment to collect an answer.

"Yes, of course I have. Every week in Sunday school growing up, I opened the Bible and read along with the teacher. Why do you ask?"

"Did you ever read my teachings on hate?" he continued his inquisition.

"I'm not sure I understand what you mean."

"It's an easy question, Diana. Did you ever read anything I taught on the subject of hate?"

She paused.

"I'm sure I have. I don't remember exactly what it said, though."

He walked past her and folded his arms near the adjoining window leaning against the glass.

"Your father was a failure in your mind, I know. Do you think that you ever hated him?"

"I suppose so," she muttered.

"Do you still?"

He might as well have punched her. The question slapped her across the face. She didn't even know what to say. Moving toward the couch again, she plopped down and stared into the fire. The sky outside was turning red at a gradual pace as the sun was waking up.

"Diana?"

"I suppose so," she repeated.

"What about Jim?"

"What about him?" she snapped back. "Do you want to know if I hate him too? Well, I do. And why shouldn't I?"

"He did hurt you really bad, didn't he? Marital affairs are always painful."

"And with the babysitter!" she screamed. "How could he do something like that with the babysitter?"

"I'm not here, Diana, to answer the question why. I want to show you how."

"How to what?" she asked, standing and facing the host.

"How to forgive."

"Forgive?" she retorted with a huff. "You're kidding, right?"

"You have so much anger and pain hidden in your heart right now that it has made you a very bitter woman. That anger and pain has developed into hate. And hate, Diana, is just as bad as murder in my Father's eyes. If you want to figure out a way to find peace in your heart, you must learn to forgive those two men, and that peace can only be found in me."

She turned from him and walked aimlessly around the room. Forgiving Jim and her father was never an option in her mind. They owed her. They owed her big time.

Chapter 17

The next morning after breakfast found the three remaining guests waiting anxiously in the lobby. Diana had not slept all night but remained up talking more with Jesus. Strangely enough, though, she felt completely rested as if she had slept for a good eight hours.

He had stayed up with her and explained his forgiveness that he offered for her own life. If she would accept that forgiveness, out of her thankfulness and joy, she would see that forgiving others was a feasible idea. It sounded farfetched, but Diana found herself lying on a couch repeating their conversation over and over in her head.

Can I really forgive them? she thought. *And do I even want to? Is there a purpose for it?*

They hadn't seen Jesus all morning, but she knew he would show up soon. She was sure that he had much more to say.

And with that thought he came walking into the room from the outside. They all gave him a strange look.

"Did you just come from outside?" Charles asked.

"Yes I did."

"I didn't know that was allowed," piped in Madison from across the room.

Jesus smiled. "I never said that you couldn't leave. I just don't recommend it."

"Can I go outside?" asked Diana.

Jesus looked at the front door. "If you walk out that door, you will walk right back into your life. And you will leave not having chosen what

I prepared for you. There is always the option to leave, but I plead with you to hear me out. Eternal consequences will be faced if you walk through that door."

Charles continued his pacing, scratching his head and shaking it.

"Are you troubled?" Jesus asked him.

Without stopping his pacing, he replied, "Well, I'm more open to the thought of a supreme being. The things you showed me blew my mind. I wanted to just label what I saw as a great illusion, but something in the back of my mind wouldn't allow me to. There could be a God.

With a nervous grin, he continued, "And for me to say that is a big deal."

"Let me take you on a ride into history," said Jesus, starting to slide one couch behind another. "It may open your eyes to more answers that have bewildered you in your science career. Come sit."

Jesus had arranged two couches in the middle of the room facing the same way, one behind another. Charles sat next to Jesus on the front couch while Madison, along with Fern, and Diana took the back couch. She felt like she was a child again pretending they were in a car.

Immediately the room went completely dark. All that was left in view were the many pictures on the walls now glowing and seeming to float on every side of them. They slowly began to spin sideways, circling the seated group. Madison gasped and grabbed onto Diana's leg. She winced with pain and took the young lady's hand into her own.

"One of the greatest questions throughout history is how did everything come to be. Everybody has come to an agreement on one thing in all of the debates. That is that something has to be eternal, whether it's a god or a strongly charged particle, or whatever they come up with. Something just can't come out of nothing. Do you agree, Charles?"

"Yeah," was all he could reply.

The pictures sped up and were now spinning rapidly around the group until they became a blur. With a bright flash, the pictures all shot out into the distance and became many twinkling stars. Although Diana was fairly sure the couch wasn't moving, the illusion that they were made her free hand grab the arm of the furniture.

A huge white planet floated before them, shining in the sunlight that came from behind them. The beauty of it left them all in silence for a while. Charles looked back at the women behind him.

"Imagine seeing this without the couches."

Jesus laughed. Diana couldn't imagine that. Charles had not described the experience justly, although she was sure any attempt would have failed.

"What planet is that?" questioned Charles. "I've never seen anything like it."

"That," Jesus answered, "is Earth; the very planet that you call your own."

Diana frowned and gave Madison a very confused look, who returned to her the same bewildered appearance. It was almost humorous how tight she was holding Fern as she stared at everything around her.

"Earth?" exclaimed Charles. "How is that Earth? Are you showing us the future? Are we going to freeze up into a world-wide ice age?"

Jesus shook his head. "No, this is the past. This is what your planet looked like from space right after I created it. The white you see is a cold, crystallized water layer that circled the planet above the atmosphere."

Diana couldn't see Charles's face but she could only imagine how fast his brain was trying to comprehend what he was hearing. He was again scratching his head and started his next question five times before it came out.

"I've never heard of this. Why should I believe you?"

Jesus again laughed. "I am not going to make you believe me, Charles. I'm here simply to show you the facts. You can do with them what you want."

Turning to the white planet, again he continued, "I separated the waters with the expanse of the sky. I created a paradise for all living things to live in. This white layer shielded humans from the harmful rays of the sun and increased the air pressure. It also provided a perfect tropical atmosphere year round."

"But that layer isn't there anymore," Charles commented.

"No, it's not," Jesus said. "But we aren't to that part yet."

Immediately the darkness went away and they found themselves in a lush, beautiful forest with tall, blossoming bushes and massive trees.

Diana spotted a giant muscular elephant making its way through the grass as if showing off its massive body to whoever would give him attention. Madison tugged on her sleeve, pointing to a meerkat only a few yards away from where she was sitting.

Animals started appearing from all directions. Diana was lost in the wonder of it all. Out of all the zoos that she had ever visited, no place had captivated her as much as here. The chirping of birds hidden somewhere in the trees, the vibrant colors of the blossoms surrounding her, and the awesome presence of the creatures all made her feel like when she was a little girl watching Animal Planet or reading through one of her many animal picture books.

Madison and Diana both gasped simultaneously as the ground beneath them started shaking. It wasn't an earthquake. It seemed more like giant footsteps coming very near to the group.

Very tense, Charles leaned over to Jesus and asked barely audible for Diana to hear, "What is that?"

Jesus just watched ahead and smiled.

"It's one of my creations. I want you to see it. It's magnificent!"

A gigantic lizard appeared, its long, muscular neck swinging back and forth. It stopped and stretched to the top of the tallest tree next to it and began to rip off the vegetation.

Diana couldn't peel her eyes away from the colossal monster. She leaned forward and asked, "What is that, Charles?"

He shrugged. "I'm in astronomy. I recognize it from pictures, but I don't have a name."

"Today people know it as Diplodocus," stated Jesus.

The enormous animal continued on its way shaking the earth as it walked. From behind some trees ran a man dressed in skins holding the hand of a boy. They avoided the massive dinosaur's footsteps and watched it walk by.

"Who are they?" questioned Madison.

"Are we in some movie or something?" Charles asked at the same time.

"No, we are in the past," explained Jesus. "I'm showing you my creation."

"But dinosaurs lived millions of years before men did," stated Charles quite matter-of-factly.

"Did they?" asked Jesus, raising one of his eyebrows. "I know for a fact that they didn't."

"How do we know that this is real?" inquired Diana, watching the man chop down a tree with what looked like a metal sort of axe. "How do we know this is really the past and not some show that you are putting on?"

Jesus remained silent for a bit. "Well I suppose you are going to have to trust me on this one. And you should trust me on this since I am the only one on these couches that is here when it happened."

"Was here," corrected Madison.

"No, is here," restated the host. "I was here all along. I just brought you here to join me."

Charles frowned at him, along with the other two guests.

"I thought you were at the hotel with us," he declared.

"I am. Madison, Fern, Diana, and you are the only ones that left the hotel to go on this journey. You just met me here."

"Huh?" they all asked.

Jesus laughed. "All of you are held in submission to time. In fact, I created it for the entire human race. But it is one of my creations. I am outside of time. I am at all times all of the time."

They all were silent. Diana's mind was racing trying to figure out what he had meant. She pondered it while watching the boy try to cut down a tree like the older man. He swung and swung, rarely hitting the same place twice.

"Okay," said Charles, interrupting the quietness. "You claim that dinosaurs lived with man. I would agree if they were still around. We are obviously still living but they are nowhere to be found. Explain that."

"I will, but I'm not sure you will enjoy it."

He didn't respond but gave Jesus a look that gave him permission to continue.

"These people that I created eventually hated me. Every thought and inclination of their hearts was evil all the time. They thought they knew better than I did on how to live their lives. With a regretful heart, I knew that they made their decision. Choosing to live apart from me only leads to one thing, death. So that's what I gave them."

"You killed all the people?" muttered Madison.

"Not all of them," answered Jesus, repositioning himself to look at the women behind him. "There was one man I chose to continue the human race. He, his wife, his three sons, and their wives were going to be the sole survivors of my wrath."

"Wait!" exclaimed Diana. "Don't tell me that you are talking about Noah. I know it's in the Bible, but that story sounds so farfetched. I always had a hard time believing that it really happened. I mean, every animal was on one boat! Give me a break!"

"Every kind of animal, Diana. That is a big difference from every animal; one kind of dog, cat, ape, etc. You get the point. But yes, I am talking of Noah. I destroyed the earth with a catastrophic flood."

He stopped talking and cleared his throat.

Turning again, he looked at Charles. "Let me show you what happened to the dinosaurs."

The couches shot upward into the sky like a sickening carnival ride. Diana's knuckles turned white as she gripped the arm of the chair.

"Don't worry. You are perfectly safe," comforted Jesus. "We aren't really moving. I'm just showing you things."

Madison mumbled with a squeaky voice, "It sure feels like we are moving."

The couches were soon high above the earth. Diana looked at the vast area of land that she could see from the high altitude. No clouds were in sight, so she could see for hundreds of miles. Beautiful, rich forests, rivers running from shore to shore, and the sun dancing off the waves of the ocean diverted her attention from her fear of heights.

"This is the day that it all happened."

Charles slowly looked at the man seated next to him.

"Should I even ask what you what you are referring to?"

Suddenly ear-piercing cracks rumbled through the atmosphere as Diana watched the large continent break across its fault lines. Large amounts of water gushed from underneath the land, mowing over anything in its path. A loud sound above her grabbed her attention as she saw a wall of water falling from the sky. Instinctively she threw her hands over her head and ducked as the water rushed by her toward the once-beautiful earth below.

Untouched by the falling water, she watched the water from above crash against the land in a greater downpour than she had ever seen before while the water from underneath ripped open the earth as if trying to meet the falling water head on.

The once rich and flourishing woodland and forests were soon under a great sea. Giant trees were being tossed in the raging sea just as a toothpick might in a mighty river.

Diana pried her eyes away from the horrific scene to look at the man who supposedly orchestrated this whole disaster. The man had his head resting on the back of the couch looking up into the sky above them. Tears were streaming down his face just about as fast as the water had fallen from the sky.

She had heard about Noah and the ark dozens of times as a child, but this scene never crossed her mind. The thought of thousands, maybe millions of people down there in that storm made her sick. She searched hard for the ark, but apparently it wasn't in eyeshot.

"Can we go back to the hotel?" cried Madison, holding Fern so tight that Diana thought she was going to suffocate her.

"Yes, that would be fine," he answered.

They all found themselves back in the calmness of the hotel lobby. They all exhaled a long breath and relaxed slightly from their journey.

Chapter 18

The silence when they returned was deafening. But even so, Diana never thought the lobby of the hotel would ever be so comforting. She had only been there a few days, but compared to the worldwide catastrophe that she had just witnessed, the leather furniture, roaring fire, and long, flowing drapes welcomed her back like old friends.

"So the dinosaurs missed the boat, eh?"

Jesus finished wiping his eyes and answered the bewildered scientist.

"Oh no, they were on the ark. Baby ones, of course; the ark wasn't that big." He forced a laugh, but nobody else joined in.

"As you know, Charles, lizards never stop growing their entire lives. But now that the water layer above the Earth was gone, the harmful rays of the sun made it through and that perfect tropical climate was no longer. Plus the air pressure wasn't great enough to support such a large animal. The Earth was now under extreme changes. Every living creature lived a shorter life span. So the lizards that once lived for hundreds of years were only living for a few years now. Since they lived for fewer years, they had fewer years to grow. The dinosaurs, as you call them, will never be as big as they were back then."

Another silence followed the host's explanation. All that could be heard was the crackling flames and the soft breathing of the sleeping baby. Diana never ceased to be amazed at what Fern could nap through.

"Well you sure do have all the answers," Charles finally retorted. "I can't argue with you scientifically apparently. That has never happened to me before. I can usually win any science debate, but you are beyond my knowledge."

He paused.

"I believe I'm ready to admit that there is a God. This is a big moment," he said, leaning in toward Jesus. "I've never believed that before."

"It is a big moment," Jesus repeated.

"But ..."Charles continued. "But I have a feeling you want me to do more than that."

"Believing I am God is a great start, Charles. But it can't end there. You are still in a very depraved state. You read that letter I gave you. Your belief needs to evolve from just knowledge to faith. Even with your admittance, you still need to put your trust in me."

"I don't get it, though!" Charles exclaimed, causing Diana to jump. "Louis obviously needed you. Courtney was a scared little girl that needed guidance. Even Harvey was a lonely old man that wanted a close friend. You were the answer to the hole in their lives."

"And your life doesn't have holes, I take it?" Jesus asked.

"I have a beautiful wife who loves me, respectful and obedient children, my dream home, a job I love and am succeeding in, and more friends then I could ever need. I can't honestly see where you fit in. Many people need you. I get that. But I'm not one of them."

Jesus looked down and breathed a sigh. Madison got up from the couch and paced the room with the sleeping baby. Diana didn't move. The intensity of the conversation and the anticipation of how Jesus would respond left her frozen in place.

"There seems to be a theme to all of the good things in your life."

Charles also stood and walked to another couch. Turning to face Jesus, he leaned against it.

"And what is that, if I dare to ask?" he asked with a hard stare.

"You," Jesus answered.

The man's hard stare became an inquisitive and confused look.

"What do you mean?"

Jesus looked back at him and replied, "Everything revolves around you. Your wife is beautiful to *you*, she loves *you*, your children respect *you*, it's *your* dream house ... you get the picture. The only reason your life doesn't have holes is because you are happy. What happens tomorrow if you lose that job, or that house, or tragically, one of your family members?"

Charles didn't answer the question. He simply looked down, watching his shoe scuff against the carpet. Diana could tell Jesus was wearing the man down.

"Charles, life isn't about you. You may think that life is grand right now because you have no worries in the world, but I beg to differ. You and I don't have a relationship right now, and that leaves you with a lot to worry about. What would happen if you died tonight? Do you think that your successful life is going to impress me so much I will just let you into heaven? I told you the prerequisite. Placing your faith in me and trusting me to cleanse you of your sins is the *only* way."

Jesus's emphasis of the word drew Charles's gaze back up to his own.

"And then I'll praise you like the birds, huh?" Charles mumbled.

Jesus laughed. "Charles, you are going to worship me whether you like it or not. I do recommend you volunteering the effort, though."

"So you will forgive me of my sins and then I praise you because of the joy and the peace and the forgiveness you have shown me? Is that how it works?"

Diana didn't like the tone that Charles had. She didn't know why, but it almost made her angry. Jesus had to have noticed as well, but his expression and demeanor never changed. He remained calm and collected, ignoring any sarcasm coming from the other man in the room.

"Yes, my people praise me for the many blessings I have showered upon them. It's how they say thank you. But it's not the main reason they adore me. Even if I never blessed them with peace, joy, love, or forgiveness, they would still praise me."

"And why would they do that?"

Jesus answered, "Because I am God. I am the Creator and Sustainer of all things. I am the only one worthy of receiving such love and adulation and respect. As I said before, all people will one day see me for who I really am, and they will declare me as Lord, and they will humbly bow before me. Those who rejected me all their lives will one day see me and they will worship. And they will not be praising me because of forgiveness or peace. They will worship because they just beheld the majesty and glory of the Living God. Unfortunately for them, it will be too late and they will be cast out of my presence. That's why, Charles, I recommend you begin worshipping me now before it's too late."

Tears began to form in the scientist's eyes.

"Jesus, I believe what you are saying is true. Everything has made sense and even clarified things in my mind. You have filled in the blanks of many things I didn't understand even as a professional astronomer. But ..."

The man swallowed and continued. "To give my life over has been a tough process. I never thought you existed, and now my mind is bombarded with the reality that there is a God."

Jesus nodded. "Your heart has been hard toward me for forty-five years. That's a tough thing to break through and change. I've been working on your heart for a long while now. That's why you are willing to listen to me."

Charles laughed nervously. "That probably would be the only way for me to do so."

"I drew you to myself because I love you. Are you ready to love me in return?"

Charles simply nodded.

"Why don't you head upstairs, Charles?"

The man rose up and walked quickly toward the door.

"Good-bye, Charles," Madison said softly.

He looked back and smiled as he disappeared behind the dining room door.

Chapter 19

Diana curled her feet under herself as she sat back into the cushion of the leather sofa. As it had been for the past few days, her mind was racing with confusion, excitement, and bewilderment. The rude and arrogant man she met at the corner had just walked out of the room completely changed. She was aware of the change in Charles as she witnessed the men's conversation. The man was different now and strangely, deep inside her heart, she was envious of who he had become.

"Aren't you going to lead him down the hallway to the others?" Madison asked Jesus.

He smiled, "I am."

Madison rolled her eyes and sighed. "Of course you are. Why wouldn't you be? I mean, you are sitting right here in front of me. Why wouldn't you be with Charles at the same time? I mean, you are God."

Jesus laughed out loud, causing a snicker to escape from Diana. Even Madison chuckled as she rested her shaking head in her hand.

"If we were on a reality show, we'd being doing great," Diana chimed in with a hint of sarcasm.

Jesus nodded. "That's true."

His face went solemn, and he stared into her eyes.

"But the fact of the matter is this isn't a game. And being the last two doesn't mean anything. The only thing that matters is what you decide here tonight; whether you will trust me with your life or continue to live as if I don't exist."

Diana attempted to gnaw on her fingernails, but there weren't any left. She dropped her hand back into her lap and looked up at the host, whose gaze was shifting from one of the women back to the other.

"I don't want to forgive Jim!"

The words blurted out before Diana knew that they were even coming. But it was exactly how she felt and why she was fighting this man sitting before her. If becoming a Christian meant forgiving a jerk like her husband, then it wasn't for her. He deserved nothing from her but what she gave him, a slap in the face and a boot out the door.

"Forgiveness is never easy, Diana," he continued. "While I hung on the cross for your sins, the deep bond that my Father and I shared was broken. You have lived your whole life apart from him, so you don't know the difference. But for eternity past we were one. But that one was severed because you were my enemy. My love for you overrode the deep anguish I felt about what I was about to go through. I wanted you to love me and have a relationship with me, and I was willing to spend three days of hell to bring about that possibility. I forgave you, Diana, even though you put me to death. Why can't you forgive your husband for a few months of infidelity?"

"Because I'm not perfect like you. I can't."

"Exactly. You aren't perfect. But you could be. Just believe I'm God, Diana. Believe I died and rose again. Put your trust in me. You have nothing to lose. Your life is falling apart, and everything in you is angry and miserable. Just give it all to me. I will help you through."

He turned to Madison. "Madison, you have some forgiveness to do as well. There are some ladies that hurt you badly, and it would be a huge stepping stone in your life if you let that bitterness and rage go."

Madison avoided his stare and petted the top of Fern's head.

"Madison, you know it wasn't me that kicked you out of that church. I love you and want to help guide you into making better decisions in your life. You will only continue to make mistakes if I'm not in your life. Believe me."

"They don't deserve forgiveness. You know that," she finally said.

"Neither do you, Madison."

Her face dropped again.

He continued. "You are not forgiving them because they deserve it. Those that are forgiven much will forgive much. It's how it works. I think you two ladies need to head up to your rooms. You both have a lot to think about."

—

The walk up the stairs seemed longer than usual as Diana contemplated his words. Louis, Courtney, Harvey, and Charles all came into her mind. They believed him. Why couldn't she?

Madison touched her shoulder as Diana turned to head into her bedroom.

"Diana, please don't leave me. We are the last two. I don't want to be left alone with him. I'm not sure what I want to believe yet."

Diana turned and hugged the young woman.

"I'm not going anywhere, hon. Don't worry."

Madison faced her microphone and quietly spoke into it.

"I can't provide a home for Fern like I had growing up."

She turned the knob and walked into her room.

Diana turned and spoke as well, "I'm not good enough."

She opened her door and stepped inside but gasped at the sight in front of her. Her waterbed was nowhere in sight. The stuffed animal heads had disappeared. In fact, she wasn't inside at all. The door behind her had disappeared and what loomed in front of her made her stomach turn upside down.

Chapter 20

Madison began to nurse Fern after sitting on her futon.

"What do I do, baby?" she asked Fern, looking down at her daughter.

Fern didn't seem to hear her but just continued to eat. Part of Madison really wanted to give God and this church thing another chance. The mystery of the place enchanted her, but it was his words that really struck her to the core. Ever since he entered her life, every time he spoke, her heart raced and her mind concentrated on every word. When she met him during that first dinner seemed so long ago now.

Her thoughts were flooded with memories from the past few days. The host seemed so loving and kind, and yet, the things he said made her deathly afraid. She had originally tried church to find friends and answers to the questions she had in life. All she found were more problems and people she wished she'd never met. But now Jesus had taught her what church was really about, and that even scared her.

After Fern was done eating, Madison picked her up and walked out of her room. She didn't know quite where she was headed, but sitting around made her think too much. Knocking on Diana's door, she waited for a response.

She must be showering or asleep, she thought.

Turning, she walked down the hallway to the invisible wall. Scrunching up her face and squinting her eyes, she tried desperately to see what was past the transparent barrier but to no avail.

"Charles!" she yelled into the darkness.

She didn't expect an answer and didn't receive one. Her head rested against the wall, and she sighed. She never liked Charles, but she felt much more comfortable when he was around. Never had she experienced such loneliness.

Walking the length of the hallway again, she stopped at the top of the spiral stairs. The lights were out downstairs, but she could picture the dining room still set up with its grand table and seven chairs perfectly spaced apart surrounding it.

Madison pictured the starving homeless man waiting for the permission to eat; the drool by the side of his mouth and his darting eyes like a child scoping out the presents under the tree on Christmas morning. The thought brought a small smile to her face as she again turned and paced the hallway.

Fern became limp in her arms, and her thin blond hair bounced with each step Madison took. The baby was beginning to get heavy, so Madison decided to take her back to the room. After entering the room, she placed the sleeping child in her crib and covered her with a blanket.

As she showered, her mind went back to her parents and her upbringing. Her dad and mom had convinced her that the goal of life was to be successful and happy. They had always been very encouraging and supportive in all she did, from sports to graduation to receiving her degree in business.

"Daddy," she whispered through her tears. "I'm not happy. I'm not happy."

Wrapped in a towel, she lay down upon the bed and sobbed. All of the anger, fear, and sadness that had controlled her over the years seemed to be escaping through her tears.

"I'm so sick of being afraid! I'm so tired of being alone!"

Her screams woke up Fern, who Madison immediately tended to. A sharp knock on the door made her jump.

"C'mon, not now," she complained under her breath.

She yelled at whoever was behind the door. "Can we talk later? I'm not even dressed!"

Again a sharp knock shook the door, and then whoever it was walked away as Madison could hear their footsteps fade down the hallway.

Frowning, she laid Fern back down and cracked open her door. On the floor at her feet was one lone sheet of notebook paper.

Chapter 21

A slight breeze struck her face as she stared in fear at the house she was standing in front of. The brick building sat there daring her to take another step. Diana turned around and saw that she was back in her neighborhood. In the distance, she could see the turn off that would lead to her driveway. Facing the wretched house once more, she turned to leave.

"I forgave you, Diana, even though you put me to death. Why can't you forgive your husband for a few months of infidelity?"

Jesus's words echoed back in her head.

"Oh, is that what this is about?" Diana asked out loud. "You think I'm going to march right into that house and forgive that woman?"

His words again came to mind.

"I forgave you, Diana, even though you put me to death."

She took a deep breath. Diana knew that this was something she had to do. The extreme anger that was dwelling inside of her wasn't going to help her get her life back. What Jesus had commanded her to do was not going to be easy, but she knew that it was necessary. She hadn't faced Rachel since the day she had confronted her about the affair. There had been much yelling and cursing, and Diana had kicked her out of the house. She didn't know if Jim had seen her again, and she had her suspicions that he had.

"Okay, God, I really want to regain the happiness I once had and maybe even get my family back together. If this is what it takes, help me.

She walked through the gate and up to the door that separated her from the woman who had destroyed her life. She took a deep breath and knocked. Hoping that nobody would answer, she knocked one more time.

The door opened, and she stood face to face with her once-trusted babysitter. Rachel's face went pale, and she said nothing. Diana stumbled over some words, but nothing intelligible came out.

Finally she spoke. "May I come in?"

The young woman still taken aback stepped aside to allow Diana into the house. The living room was cluttered with stacked books, boxes of clothes, and various other items all over the floor.

"Please excuse the mess," she apologized. "I'm cleaning out the closets."

Diana turned and faced the woman. "I'm not sure why I'm here ... I mean, I know why I'm here ... but I don't know how ..."

Flustered she took another breath.

"May we sit?"

"Of course," Rachel answered, gesturing to a long couch against the opposite wall. "Listen, if you are here to lecture me again, it's not necessary. I know it was wrong, and a day hasn't gone by that I don't regret it. I've wanted to apologize to you, but I thought the last thing you would want is to see me."

Diana sat staring at the floor listening to her. She couldn't believe she was here, but she knew that this was going to be the starting block to regaining her life.

"Rachel, I'm not here to lecture you. The last few days have been very interesting for me, and I know now that I need to do something. What Jim and you did to me has eaten at me since the day I found out. It has made me into a very bitter and angry woman, and I'm sick of it. I need to start moving on with my life."

Diana reached over and held young woman's hand, which was now trembling.

"I forgive you, Rachel. I can clearly see that you are sorry for what you did, but even if you weren't, I forgive you."

Rachel began to weep uncontrollably. Her face was buried in her free hand, and she gasped between sobs. Diana's eyes were watering now as well, and she leaned in to the sorrowful woman and embraced her.

"Rachel, you were the best babysitter that I ever had. The kids adored you, and you worked with such integrity. I felt betrayed by you. You took advantage of my trust and stole my husband from me. But I need to begin to fix what has been broken, and I can't do that with the hate I felt for you still in my heart. I do care for you and am heartbroken for you. It will be something that you will have to live with for the rest of your life, but you too can move past it and learn from it. I don't know what will happen between Jim and me, but I'm working on forgiving him as well."

Rachel's body was still shaking from her violent sobbing, but she caught her breath and looked into Diana's eyes.

"I'm so sorry. It was never my intention. It just happened. I make no excuses for it because I am to blame. But I am so, so sorry. I miss your family terribly, and it kills me to know that the relationship will never be the same."

"Me too," agreed Diana.

Rachel smiled. "Thank you. I don't know how you knew to come today, but this mess in my house is a result from the unrest in my mind. Cleaning is how I deal with stress and grief. For some reason today, the weight of the guilt poured down on me. Suicide even crossed my mind, Diana. Suicide! I never thought that would be me."

Diana began to cry even harder. She understood why God had sent her to Rachel's house today. A chill shot down her spine as she realized that she had almost walked away from this house, and she didn't want to think what would have happened if she had.

"God can forgive you for what you have done," continued Diana, still holding Rachel, who was now getting control of her sobs.

"God?" questioned the young woman, shooting a confused look her direction. "I didn't know that you believed in God."

"I told you, it's been an interesting few days for me. Before you can get right with me or anybody else, you need to deal with him. I've been reminded that I've been forgiven for much in my life, and that is what has helped me forgive you. I know that all my wrongdoings and selfishness nailed Jesus to the cross, but he died purposefully to give me new life. I want the same for you."

Rachel shook her head. "Don't get me wrong, Diana, what you just did for me meant the world. But I'm not ready to figure out what I want to do with God yet."

"A few days ago, I felt the same way. I trust soon that you will know what to do with him. He's real, Rachel, and waiting for you to take his gift. I took the gift, and it's the best thing I've ever done."

Chapter 22

There are those who dwelt in darkness and in the shadow of death, prisoners in misery and chains, because they had rebelled against the words of God and spurned the counsel of the Most High. Therefore He humbled their heart with labor. They stumbled and there was none to help. Then they cried out to the Lord in their trouble. He saved them out of their distresses. He brought them out of the darkness and the shadow of death and broke their bands apart.

Let them give thanks to the Lord for his lovingkindness and for His wonders to the sons of men!

Madison read it three times before closing the door behind her again. Sitting on the bed, she read it two more times.

Then they cried out to the Lord in their trouble. He saved them …

"Jesus!" she screamed, not caring about waking up Fern. "Jesus, am I supposed to cry out to you now! These words seem to be describing me. Is that what I'm supposed to do? I should just cry out to you now?

She breathed slowly and began again.

"I know I need you. I need you to help me raise Fern. I don't know what I'm doing. In fact, I don't know what I'm doing with my life! It's falling apart. My life is literally the shadow of death. Jesus …"

Anger raced through her, and she stood, crumpling the paper in her hands, and threw it at the door. It bounced lightly off the wall and rolled under the crib. Running into the hallway, she screamed. Everything that had been bottled up inside of her suddenly erupted.

"Jesus, where are you?" she exclaimed. "When I need you, you aren't here! Where are you!"

She fell to her knees and buried her face in her lap.

"Madison, my child, I'm right here. I'll always be here for you."

Her head shot up and looked around. Nobody was with her in the hall.

"Where are you?" she again asked.

"I told you, I'm with you. Just because you can't see me doesn't mean that I have left you. I am with you always. Your pain is so evident to me, and I'm begging you to give it to me.

"Why the letter? Why can't you just come tell me yourself?"

"Those are my words. Those words are exactly what you needed to hear tonight. You felt like a prisoner in your own body, lost in the dark. I am waiting here to be your Savior, the one who will break the chains that have been keeping you from truly living life. Will you trust in me and let me free you?"

Madison couldn't say anything. A huge knot formed in her throat, and she took a moment and swallowed it. Her heart was burning in her chest. This was the time. Earlier, she silently had mocked the other four who followed this Jesus. But now she understood why they had given their lives to him. She had nothing left. He was willing to take her miseries and darkness and bring her salvation. People had failed, not God. She realized that now.

"Jesus, please come to me. I have nothing to offer you except my brokenness and confusion. Please do what you will with me. I've messed up my life no matter how hard I have tried to do something right. Only you can get me out. Please, come."

A loud bang sounded behind her as she jumped to her feet and spun around. Jesus was walking toward her from down the hallway. A large smile filled his face as he reached her and wrapped her in his arms. She clung to him and buried her face in his chest.

"There, there, Madison," he said calmly, patting her back. "The wall is now open. There is no barrier left between you and me. Care to join me?"

Jesus turned and pointed to the now-open hallway. Madison nodded and smiled. Her heart, which was pounding a few moments ago, was now calmly beating in her chest. The once-dark hall was now lit up and welcoming.

"May I take Fern with me?" she asked, heading for her bedroom door.

Jesus grabbed her arm gently.

"No, Madison, Fern will be fine here for now. Trust me. Once we are done, then you can come back and get her before you go home."

Her gaze shot up to meet the host's eyes.

"Home?" she asked. "Why would I want to go home? I am as happy as I have ever been right here with you. I don't want to leave and go back to that dark life I left a few days ago."

"But you must go home," responded Jesus. "Your life has now begun. I told you I will never leave you. And then when your work is done, I promise, you will come and live with me forever. Okay?"

She nodded. He motioned for her to follow him down the mysterious hallway.

He continued, "I am overjoyed that you have decided to give me your life. Are you ready?"

For the first time in many years, a large smile appeared across Madison's face. And this smile came from joy now overflowing in her heart.

Chapter 23

Diana gave Rachel one final hug before leaving her house. As soon as the door slammed behind her, she found herself once again in her room in the hotel. She sat on the edge of the water bed. Once again, she eyed the pictures displayed on the end table. The word "ME" caught her attention, but this time she understood. God was now the person in her life that she never knew—a family member she could trust entirely. She dropped back onto the bed and rode the waves while, staring at the great animals looming overhead.

Rap, rap, rap. The knock at the door caused her to sit up. She answered the door, and there stood Jesus with his arms out. Walking into his arms, they embraced.

"Why am I still here?" questioned Diana. "I believed you before I left for my room."

"I know you did," he replied. "But that thing you did with Rachel was really important."

"Will I be able to go down the hallway?" she asked, nodding in that direction.

"Of course!" he said with a smile. "Shall we?"

She smiled and joined him walking past the door of Louis's old room. She spun around panicked, suddenly remembering her friend.

"Wait!" she exclaimed, grabbing Jesus's arm. "What about Madison and Fern? I can't leave them here. She's not strong enough to make it by herself."

"Don't worry, child," Jesus assured her. "Madison will never be alone again. She is no longer here. While you were away, she too believed."

A huge smile spread across her face and she turned back toward the mysterious hallway very excitedly.

"Let's go!"

—

Diana jumped at the noise of the giant transparent door cracking from the top to the bottom. When the crack reached the entire height of the wall, the wall split and parted for the two to enter. Jesus began to walk, and a few moments later, Diana ran and caught up with him.

On both sides of the hallway were other doors exactly like the one that had been her bedroom here.

"There are more bedrooms?" she asked. "Are there more people here?"

She watched him as he continued to walk and just shake his head.

"No. There were many more invitations than just you six. Only the people you met actually came."

"So, there were supposed to be more people here to meet you?"

"Yes, Diana. Many are called, but few are chosen."

She looked at him inquisitively. Her mind desperately tried to wrap around what he had just said.

"Where are those people now?" she finally asked.

"Living their life exactly how it has always been. Some have people in their lives just like Lisa, constantly praying for them. Others have heard the gospel in various ways: through church, family, and strangers. But all are completely blind to the truth."

"Why don't you make them come? They need you!"

He just shook his head. "A relationship is a choice made by two people. I will not force anybody to love me. That is not true love."

They walked in silence until the last bedroom was behind them. The hallway ended at a giant door. It looked very similar to the front door of the hotel with its giant handles and grand size. Jesus walked up to the door, grabbed it with both hands, and turned to Diana and smiled.

"Prepare yourself."

As the doors swung open, singing erupted. It echoed off the walls and traveled down the hallway behind her. She seemed to be enveloped in the melody of the booming choir that Diana still couldn't see in the enormous room that Jesus led her into. Although she could not understand the words, it was an extremely joyful song. Diana found it almost frustrating to listen to since her senses couldn't totally grasp all that she was hearing. She had never heard such harmonies and voice ranges.

The room was as white as white could get. The room seemed to never end, with massive walls on each side. It seemed there were prisms hanging everywhere as various colors bounced off the walls and shot through the room. Along with all of the colors that she already knew were some others that she didn't recognize at all.

"Heaven rejoices when one person repents," Jesus said after the song had finished.

"That song was because of me?" she asked, her mouth gaping open.

He grinned and nodded, then continued walking. She followed close behind him staring at the colors still darting to and fro before her. Up ahead, positioned on a large podium in the middle of the room, Diana could see a giant book. She took a brief glance at Jesus, who was very intent on reaching it.

"Why the extremely white room with the many colors darting around?" she questioned as they walked.

"What was the first thing you noticed about the hotel when you got here?"

Diana's mind escaped back to the old school bus, the tense passengers, Chester, and the colossal hotel.

"It was made of giant rocks. The hotel seemed empty and dark. I didn't think there was anybody inside. It seemed abandoned and dead."

"The hotel resembles the heart of the person seeing it. Before you put your trust in me, your heart was hard and dead to me. You were walking in darkness and completely empty inside. Now …"

He motioned for Diana to look around her.

She smiled. "My heart is white."

"You were once dead in sin, black as death. But my blood has cleansed you and made you as white as snow. In a place that sorrow and despair once thrived, joy and peace now overwhelm."

Turning to the book, which was now sitting right before them, he began to turn the pages. Diana noticed list after list of names as he turned to the last page with writing.

"All that come to me will have their names written in the Book of Life. You are now my child, so you are included."

He lowered his gaze to the page and Diana followed it. She noticed the other guests' names on the page as well: Louis Turner Simpson, Courtney Lynn Koontz, Harvey Moore, Charles Robert Hartford, and Madison Rebeka Sooner.

"Where's Fern's name?"

Jesus shook his head. "Not yet. I hope to add her to this book later."

She continued to ask questions. "There is a blank space between Charles's and Madison's name. What is that for?"

"That's your space," he said. "It's time to add you."

Diana stared at the page as her name suddenly appeared into the space as if invisible hands were writing it. And then, in a matter of seconds, Diana Kay Newman was written beautifully in the book.

"This will never be erased," Jesus said confidently. "Come, I want to show you more."

Walking past the book, they came upon a ladder that led to a room above them. Jesus led the way and disappeared into the upstairs room. As Diana's head appeared through the hole in the floor, her eyes beheld the largest library that she had ever seen. She walked along one of the bookshelves and frowned as she scanned the books.

"They are all the same book!"

"Sure are," Jesus replied, laughing.

He walked over to one of the cases and grabbed one of the Bibles off of the shelf. Turning to Diana, he held the book out to her. She smiled and took it from his hands.

"This is mine?" she asked with a grin.

"Absolutely. You will need one to get through the rest of your life. This is the main way that I will communicate with you."

She paused. "Um, I've read some of this before when I was a girl. Some of it is really hard to understand."

Diana flipped quickly through the pages. "This whole thing is very intimidating."

Jesus nodded. "I understand that concern, but my Holy Spirit will be your teacher, and I will bring pastors and teachers into your life that will help you learn as well. I made this book easy enough to understand that even the simplest of people can grasp my gospel, but I made it complex enough that I require all my children to study."

Diana smiled. "I must have only read the complex parts then!"

They both laughed. She gazed at the man's face, so friendly and kind. She couldn't believe that at one time she had been afraid of him. Everything he did and said pointed to the fact that this was truly the Son of God. She loved him more than she had ever loved anybody else in her life. Ironically, they had only been in a relationship for a little while.

"Do I really have to leave? I mean, I miss my kids terribly and am longing to see them, but I very much want to stay here and talk with you more."

"Yes, you must go. This hotel isn't where you belong. I have things for you to do back at home. Trust me, we will spend eternity together and it will be more wonderful than this."

"How can it possibly be more wonderful than this?"

He smiled. "Because everybody who has ever put their trust in me will be there! That kind of intimate fellowship will be more wonderful than you can imagine. And it isn't as far in the future as you think."

She frowned, "What do you mean? Am I going to die soon?"

He laughed. "That's not what I'm saying at all. In my perspective, it's just around the corner. Compared to eternity, your life is but a mist. With me, Diana, you will now be able to live your life completely and fully. You have all you need. I love you and will be right here."

His finger pointed toward her chest.

"It's time for you to go, my child. There's a door just beyond that bookcase. It will bring you back to where you came from. You must go. People need you."

She hugged him as tears poured from the corners of her eyes. She was sad and yet extremely excited at the same time. Thoughts of her children and a new relationship with her mom and Jim came to her. She knew that life was going to be hard, but she couldn't wait to start.

She opened the door, and a breeze swept by her, sending a chill down her body. She took one final look back. Jesus was nowhere to be seen. She took a deep breath and stepped through the door.

Chapter 24

She opened her eyes and read her cell phone: 6:46. Confused, she looked around her. Down a couple of blocks she saw the corner, Sixth and North. She was leaning against the light pole, just as she had days ago. And yet, checking her cell phone again, it wasn't days later.

"What?" was all she could get out. Her hand squeezed something. Looking down, she saw the Bible that had been given to her in the library. She again fixed her eyes on the now-beloved corner where she had met her Savior, but something was wrong. People were running around and screaming. Gasping, she recognized Harvey's white Jaguar crashed into a tree.

After running a block toward the scene, an ambulance screamed past her as two police cars had already parked near the accident. Cops, EMTs, and civilians were all working together to get the driver out of the crashed vehicle. She continued running until she was only about ten yards from the wrecked sports car. She stopped, stood, and watched the chaos.

It took only a few minutes for the crew to remove the lifeless driver from the mangled Jaguar and place him carefully out on the pavement. One of the medical team was kneeling over him checking all of his vitals. He sat back on his heels and shook his head. Diana watched helplessly as a white sheet was placed over Harvey.

A peace came over her as she remembered Harvey talk about his beloved Annie and how much he missed her. Jesus had assured them that Annie was with him and when Harvey died, he had died knowing Jesus for the first time. Harvey didn't want to die alone, and what he got instead was life eternal with Christ. Her grief for his death turned to envy as she realized that Harvey was walking and talking with that mysterious host of the hotel. She couldn't wait for her turn.

She turned and began the walk home. Jesus had told her that she had work to do until that would happen. She picked up her cell phone and dialed the first person who should know about her change.

"Hello."

"Hi, Lisa. I know you are at work, but I needed to call you."

"That's fine, babe, I just left for lunch. I'm fighting this darned traffic right now."

"Well, it's hard to explain. I feel like I've been gone for days, but I know I haven't. Yesterday I was so discouraged and you told me that you were praying for me. Well he heard you."

There was a long pause.

"What does that mean? Who heard me?" Lisa asked slowly.

"I met Jesus today. He answered a lot of my questions, and I eventually gave my life to him. I realized I was living in fear and couldn't raise my family like I needed to without his guidance. Lisa, I'm a Christian now. And now that I know what it's all about, I can see why you were talking to me about him so much."

There was another long pause and then a scream.

"Aaahhh! Really!" Lisa questioned. "You are a Christian! You met Jesus! Oh, Diana, I'm so excited right now. Meet me at my house. I'm going to call work and tell them I can't come in for the rest of the day. We have so much to catch up on!"

"Okay, okay," Diana said, laughing.

She loved how emotional Lisa got over things. And this time she understood completely. How Lisa was reacting was exactly how Diana felt on the inside. She couldn't think of a better person to spend the rest of the day with than her best friend and now, sister in Christ.

"I'll be there in an hour, Lisa. I have a couple of other things I need to do first."

"Okay, babe! See you then!"

Diana sat down on her couch and laid her head back against the cushion. Duke sprawled out at her feet and nudged her with his nose until she began to rub his stomach with her foot. She called Jim's house and asked for John.

"Hey John, how are things?"

"Good," was all he said.

"I heard you were going to the zoo. Are you excited for that?"

"Uh, how did you hear about it?"

She laughed. "Kara must have told me."

"I suppose. It's kind of hot out. It should be okay, though. Kara is bouncing around the house right now. We were supposed to leave fifteen minutes ago. I'm not supposed to talk long on the phone."

Diana laughed and John joined in. She loved his laugh.

"Well I just wanted to call and say I love you."

"I love you too, Mom."

"Why don't you tell your father hi for me?"

"Really? Why?"

"Why not? He is still my husband. Have fun!"

"Bye, Mom."

—

Diana went upstairs to her bedroom and placed her new Bible onto her pillow. Walking into her bathroom, she bent over the sink and washed her face. Looking up into the mirror as she dried herself, she noticed a difference in her eyes. She was definitely not the same person she had been the night before.

"Thank you, Jesus. I know you are right here. I love you. Help me to do what I'm supposed to do."

Chapter 25

The high school graduation had lasted for two hours, and Jim collapsed into his recliner, exhausted. He was so proud of his son for graduating with honors and how he had received three scholarships. Even though he wouldn't have missed it for the world, it was extremely miserable in the gym that was crammed full beyond capacity.

He got up and walked into the kitchen for a glass of water. As he filled the glass, the telephone rang. He sat down the glass and ran for the phone, which had fallen out of his pocket into the chair.

"Hello."

"Hello, Mr. Newman?"

"Yes, this is him."

"Yes, Mr. Newman, this is a very good friend of Diana's. She has been asking us to meet for years now. I have helped her through a lot and she thought our meeting would be a good idea."

"She did, huh. Why would I want to meet one of her friends?"

"You have noticed a change in her, haven't you?"

"Well, yes. Three years ago she became very friendly toward me and constantly was telling me that she was praying for me. About a year ago, she set me down and confessed how much she had hated me. She continued on by telling me that she forgave me ... Anyways, why are you calling? Who are you?"

"So tomorrow you are going to get an invitation in the mail. It will have a time and place where you will come to meet me. I will provide you with a place to stay where you will get the much-needed rest that you have been longing for. I will also present you with a fantastic gift if you will only come and receive it."

"What if I don't come?"

"That's up to you, Jim. I hope you choose well. Remember the change in Diana. Good-bye, Mr. Newman."

CPSIA information can be obtained at www.ICGtesting.com
Printed in the USA
BVOW071924240512

291050BV00002B/51/P